- - - - - - - - -

The

Mimicking

of

Known

Successes

MALKA OLDER

The

Mimicking

of

Known

Successes

Tor Publishing Group
New York

For

Calyx   Paz   Azul

THE MIMICKING OF KNOWN SUCCESSES

Copyright © 2023 by Malka Older

A Tordotcom Book
Published by Tom Doherty Associates / Tor Publishing Group
120 Broadway
New York, NY 10271

www.tor.com

Tor® is a registered trademark of Macmillan Publishing Group, LLC.

Library of Congress Cataloging-in-Publication Data

Names: Older, Malka, 1977– author.
Title: The mimicking of known successes / Malka Older.
Description: First Edition. | New York : Tordotcom, 2023. | "A Tom Doherty Associates Book."
Identifiers: LCCN 2022041407 (print) | LCCN 2022041408 (ebook) |
    ISBN 9781250860507 (hardcover) | ISBN 9781250860514 (ebook)
Subjects: LCGFT: Novels.
Classification: LCC PS3615.L39 M56 2023 (print) | LCC PS3615.L39 (ebook) |
    DDC 813/.6—dc23/eng/20220829
LC record available at https://lccn.loc.gov/2022041407
LC ebook record available at https://lccn.loc.gov/2022041408

Our books may be purchased in bulk for promotional, educational, or business use. Please contact your local bookseller or the Macmillan Corporate and Premium Sales Department at 1-800-221-7945, extension 5442, or by email at MacmillanSpecialMarkets@macmillan.com.

First Edition: 2023

Printed in the United States of America

0 9 8 7 6 5 4 3 2 1

Demand better than back to normal

- - - - - - - -

Prologue

The man had disappeared from an isolated platform; the furthest platform eastward, in fact, on the 4°63' line, never a very popular ring. It took Mossa five hours on the railcar to get there, alone because none of her Investigator colleagues were available, or eager, to take such a long trip for what would almost certainly be confirmation of a suicide.

The platform appeared out of the swirling red fog, and moments later the railcar settled to a halt at what could barely be called a station. Mossa, who had not been looking forward to the long trip herself, had nonetheless passed it in a benevolent daze, looking out at the gaseous horizon that seemed abstractly static as it moved in constant strange patterns. Once disembarked, she found the rhythm of talking to people on the platform only with difficulty.

"And you say he was standing here?" Mossa asked.

"That's right," the settler confirmed. "Staring out into the eastern fog. People do that sometimes, no harm in it."

Mossa grunted, not quite in agreement. She was aware

that just because she didn't understand the appeal—you couldn't see a meter out into the muck anyway, what did it matter how far the ring had to curve before the next platform?—didn't mean that others wouldn't. But if you *were* emotionally inclined to find significance in that sort of thing, doing so on this platform seemed fairly likely to deepen any gloom you were feeling. The beaten metal was largely bare, the single ring crossing along it lonely, and it might have been a psychological effect of the sparse construction and distance from anywhere else on the planet, but the gasses seemed to flow high here, wraithing around them as if the platform had sunk lower than the standard height.

Maybe it had. The maintenance team didn't make it out here very often, judging from the streaks of oxidation on the ledge.

"And then?" *Did he leap? Fall?* The parapet edging the platform was the regulation height, enough to rule out any but the most outré of accidents.

"He turned and went into the pub." The settler gestured towards the stretch of platform beyond the minimal overhang that stood in for a station, where five buildings huddled into the atmosphere: four residences, with probably two or three separate homes apiece, and a pub with a home above it. The general store would come on a railcar, Mossa figured: a good long stop at the end of the line to allow the residents to select their purchases before sliding back in the other direction.

"Oh?"

"Had a lovely big breakfast. Last meal, I suppose," the settler added, with mournful satisfaction.

"And then?"

The person shrugged, most of the motion muffled by their atmoscarfs, enveloping enough to be more properly called wraps. "Didn't see him after that."

"When did you realize he was missing?"

"It was Ganal, at the pub, noticed first. Like a good pubkeep should. Then when she mentioned, 'Where's that stranger? Came in on the morning rail?' we all started looking." The settler shrugged. "Nowhere much to hide here, no railcars had been in or out, so. One way or the other, he went over."

Mossa and the settler stared down from the platform in silence, observing the constant writhe of the gaseous mixture barely below them, barely visible in the dim glow from the gaslights of the platform. At last Mossa turned away. "I'll need to speak to the pubkeep."

"Turned in now, shouldn't wonder."

Nobody wanted this to be easy. Mossa didn't want to spend any longer on this piece of grit than necessary—she certainly wasn't going to *sleep* here—but she had to at least try to find out what had happened to this mysterious stranger. "We'll have to rouse her."

The settler shrugged without surprise. "You might as well have a meal there, then. Soften her up, and give you something to do while you wait for her to be able to make sense. She only went to sleep a few hours ago, see."

The pub was cozier than she expected: stacked rows of low pipe fires burning blue along one wall and rather nice rugs piled on the floor and hanging from the walls. A rabbit lollopped under some chairs in the corner, and a partridge muttered to itself on a perch high up behind the bar.

Mossa had not wanted the food, from a reluctance to commit herself to staying any longer than absolutely necessary as well as a deep suspicion about the quality of the meal. She was surprised to enjoy it.

"Heirloom Haricots," the pubkeep said, nodding as she poured herself another swill of caffeination from her thermos. "It's not just in the name."

Mossa looked up at her, still chewing. "How did you know?"

The pubkeep lifted one round shoulder. "You had that look on your face, like you couldn't believe what you were eating."

"They are tasty."

The pubkeep nodded at a planter. "Sequenced by my ancestor as a school project. We found it buried in one of the data caches they brought on the evacuation, along with gigs of other useless stuff. You won't find the same flavor profile anywhere else on Giant."

"The rest of it's good too," Mossa said, rendered generous by the unexpected bounty.

"Had to live up to the beans." The pubkeep yawned and nodded. "Now you know, maybe you'll come out here for a meal once in a while."

Mossa nodded, although she doubted she'd ever want that taste badly enough for a five-hour rail ride each way. *Especially* if she didn't have access to an Investigator railcar and had to go public. "Tell me about the stranger," she said, putting her utensils down reluctantly.

The pubkeep yawned again, her first words squeaking

around it. "Not much to tell. He came in, ordered breakfast—the cheese slurry over green beans. I asked where he was in from, and he said Valdegeld, but kind of proud-like, you know how some of them do, and he started dropping bits about how important he was there with his work and all and he clearly wanted to be asked more 'bout it, so I didn't." The pubkeep's lined face spread in a grin, then dropped the smile just as quickly. "You don't think that's why he—"

Mossa considered the question. "People who are very pleased with themselves are rarely driven to suicide by lack of interest from a single stranger." People who were very pleased with themselves generally did not jump off of isolated platforms without an audience, either. Of course the pubkeep's character assessment might not be valid, but . . .

Valdegeld. That at least gave her a place to start. Mossa noted that her desire to return there, the specific pulls of tactile and taste memory, were balanced almost evenly by a strong emotional reluctance.

"Heh, you're right at that." The pubkeep ran a cloth over the counter for the third time, then turned to fiddle with the atmosfilter controls, though Mossa detected no anomaly in the admixture she was breathing. "I guess I did ignore him a bit. Every time I did say a word to him his answer was about how wonderful Valdegeld is, great center of learning and culture bladdabladdabladda, which isn't so much of interest, or mostly how wonderful he is, which is less so. So I let him be."

"Reasonable enough," Mossa said.

"Right. I washed up, made breakfast for myself and Loba, who usually comes in before starting his day. When I looked around again he was gone. I assumed he'd gone to do whatever he came here for." Despite the pubkeep's hopes, it seemed people did not come all this way just for the green beans.

"And how did you notice he was missing?"

Yawn. "Well, I asked around a bit. Not everyone comes in here during the day, but usually at least someone from every building on the platform, you know? And I kept asking who the stranger was visiting and what he was here for and no one knew. Every once in a while we get poets or young people who want to come out here just because it's far away from everything, although not that many because everyone knows the platforms on 0°98' go much farther east. So when I stepped outside of the pub I took a look around the platform, in case he was, you know, staring into the void or whatever they like to do. But I didn't see him. I checked whether there had been a private railcar in, but nothing since the scheduled rail in the morning. And we would see it: everything fronts on the line, you can't have something come in without people seeing. Then I asked with a bit more purpose, but nobody knew him. We couldn't find him. And then we sent the telegram to the Investigators." A pause. "Took you long enough to get out here."

Mossa understood peripheric resentment of the center, but felt no need to explain why this had been a low priority regardless. She considered redoing the interviews with the platform residents, but it was a soggy idea all around. If the locals had lied to their pubkeep, they certainly weren't going to tell her the answer. Unless the pubkeep was lying, but why would she do that and not get them to confirm her story?

"Sad," the pubkeep said. She had finished her cup and was pouring from the thermos again. "Although why someone would come all the way out here instead of stepping off their own platform I never understand, bothering others for nothing like that. But"—swerving back to guilt again—"I suppose there was nothing we could have done."

"No, of course not," Mossa said. "Nothing at all you could have done." She didn't know that, but there was no harm in saying it. And she didn't know what had happened to the stranger either, but she found her inclination was that he hadn't dropped off the edge of the settlement into the featureless and crushing gasses of the planet. Or at least, if he had, it hadn't been by choice.

Because Mossa had used a private railcar pertaining to the Investigator's collective for this trip, she was able to depart as soon as she wished. The vehicle was comfortable enough, on the basis that its users might sometimes be required to travel for long periods without particularly wanting to. It was well-heated, and there was tea available, and Mossa sat wrapped in the cushions and covers and brooded. She had turned one of the wall panels into a storyboard for the investigation, plotting the little she knew and what she wanted to find out. It didn't require a review of the paltry first and the much more extensive second to figure out where she needed to go next, however. And when she considered who might be helpful there, she found the optimal, alluring, inconvenient name immediately.

Valdegeld. And Pleiti.

Chapter 1

A strong tempest swirled in as my railcar approached Valdegeld University Platform. I was coming back after a short holiday and eager to get back to my rooms and my studies, so I watched the approach of the storm with annoyance. I could see it long before it caught us in its tendrils, the pressure changes tinting the fog orange, then pink, then fierce red, deepening as it closed with our ring, the famous 1°02' that stopped at Valdegeld's main station as well as at Trubrant and Giant's capital, Yaste. It had taken me three changes to get back from my parents' farming platform on a much less traveled ring, and I was weary. Our carriage slowed as the first ráfagas of wind shuddered it on its single rail. Then someone must have calculated we were better off risking a rush to the station rather than waiting it out sans abris, and we accelerated, speeding even past the point where the signals suggested a lenten approach to the station. I braced myself for a hard brake, but Valdegeld platform is exceedingly long, and the railcar found a stopping point with only a bit of sharpness.

The carriage continued rocking even after we stopped, the storm bullying into the platform station and shoving railcars, fog, and, from what I could see through the windows, pedestrians. I stared for a moment, enjoying the dramatic view: the fast-moving fog of the massive perturbation fit the romantic, gloomily august image of Valdegeld, an image that still entranced me long after I had officially become a resident. I gathered my atmoscarf, slung my satchel, made for the door.

There was a small cluster of faces on the andén—like petals on a branch, my Classical training interjected, even if I could not visualize *petals* with exactitude—but I wasn't expecting anyone to be waiting for me, and I gave them no more than a cursory glance, turning immediately towards the Avenue Supal exit. Storm-driven miasma curled reddish around hurrying travelers, the blank door to the waiting room, the wheeled tea kiosk, and then a face looming suddenly out of the dimness.

"Hullo, Pleiti."

I smiled automatically, then stared. For a moment I felt myself back in time, a student again, greeted by my closest friend after a short absence, but no: I was a Classics scholar, a plum position that after two years still seemed almost unbelievable luck, and I hadn't seen this face in half a decade.

"Mossa? What are you doing here?"

"Ah. Well." Mossa looked around. "Perhaps we could talk somewhere more private?"

I had almost forgotten we were standing in the middle of one of the busier stations on Giant. "Come along, then."

I led her up Supal, which hadn't changed much since Mossa and I were students: the typically curlicued lanterns; the tea shops designed for every taste from quiet to rowdy, basic to exclusive; the prayer booths in a range of denominations; the quaint bookshops in every specialization. Shops offered every need of the scholar, from magnifying eyewear to artificial lighting, tactile enhancement, containers of various stimulants, auditory recorders, atmospheric mufflers for every part of the body, hypnotic hummers, erudite guides to the university, plated reminder mechanisms. The uneven paving of the street creaked somewhat underfoot, aged and familiar, and rose steeply away from the station, allowing for the many unsightly functions of platform life to take place below the walking level. That wasn't necessary on more recent platforms, but when Valdegeld was constructed, heating, to take one example, was propounded through vast mechanisms of steam and turbine, many of which still clunked along below the quaint buildings lining the way, emitting drifts of vapor that mingled with the motley planetary fog.

The roof that covered the station had extended up to this point, shielding us from the worst of the tempest and containing a hint of warmth, but a rush of chilled yellowish fog ahead signaled the shift to the university proper. Even Mossa, always so contained, grimaced at the sight of the storm playing out across the high steeples of Valdegeld. We dashed across the open plaza, the perturbation churning gaseous clouds above around and through, and delved into the narrow alleys of the university.

The streets there were crooked and uneven, burrowing among high buildings constructed in the sinuous style of a century and a half earlier, a fashion that, though outmoded, still held a powerful enough grip on the popular imagining to thrill me every time I looked up at them. I took us up Potash Lane, a slightly less direct route to my rooms but more sheltered. I searched, as always, for the almost un-noticeable seam where inconsistencies in the surface of the platform traced the plating of an ancient satellite, snagged from its orbit and hammered flat. I loved Valdegeld's quaintness, its details of salvage and bricolage, unlike the newer, uniform platforms pressed in enormous pieces from asteroid metal. A glance at Mossa, however, told me she was feeling the cold more than any architectural appreciation or, for that matter, nostalgia, and I hastened to lead her to my rooms. We cluttered into the archway entrance, I called a quick halloo to the porter huddled in the warm lodge, and then we were up the stairs and piling into my own scholar's suite.

Automatically, I banged the switch for the fire, and cheerful blue flames leapt into existence. "Vile out," I commented, unwrapping my atmoscarf and holding my hand out for Mossa's so I could hang it up. She handed it to me and started a slow circuit of the room, examining the furnishings and accoutrements, lingering over the reproduction of a Classical atlas, the tiny cubical qibla astrolabe, the engraving of an antelope. I watched her, not without a quick internal reassessment of my decorating and comfort choices.

"Well then," I said, to distract us both. "What are you doing here?"

Mossa, I was pleased to see, looked a little ashamed. "I thought you'd suggest a café or something. But I'm glad to see your rooms. The scholar suites are—"

"What. Are you *doing here*?"

Mossa looked even more uncomfortable. "It's work."

I considered that. "I haven't done anything bad."

Mossa rolled her eyes. "Was looking for your *help*."

"Oh. With what? Wait. *My* help? What kind of help?"

Mossa sighed, loosened her jacket. "May I sit?"

I frowned at her, but she was just as chilled and damp as I was. "Oh, very well. I suppose you want tea, too?"

"And scones? I've been thinking about the university scones from the moment I turned in this direction."

I frowned more, but again, same. I touched the order buttons. "Well then?"

Mossa looked like she really needed that tea. "Something's happened that we're having trouble understanding."

"And you think *I* can help?" Mossa lifted her eyes to my stare. "Something at Valdegeld?" But there were many people at Valdegeld; would she really come to me first? "Something happened related to the Classics faculty?" I was a scholar, yes, but with only two years I was a very junior one. "Do you need an introduction to one of the University administrators? The dean of the Classics faculty, or the University rector, perhaps?" The Investigators could have gone directly to any of those people, but Mossa might prefer a more oblique route.

"Maybe." Mossa stood again, and started pacing.

Perhaps it wasn't the university. "Or," I tried, "there was a problem with the mauzooleum?"

She winced. "*Please* tell me you don't call it that."

"I'll tell you *you* best not call it that when we're speaking with the Chief Preserver, if that's who you need."

"Hardly a preserver when they were all already dead," Mossa commented, and I glared.

"You're going to argue the finer points of linguistics with *me*?"

"Why not? I thought," her voice perilously gentle, "that your job was mainly numbers."

Fortunately, at that moment, the bell rang, and I went to retrieve the scones from the dumbwaiter. "Less time than it takes for a plate of university scones," I said, setting them on the low table before the fire, "for us to quarrel." I fetched my sugar, cinnamon, cocoa, and garam masala shakers, and the pot of honey, and added them to the table. Mossa said nothing, though she did not immediately snag a scone, either. I sighed, and settled myself on the cushions to one side of the table, gesturing her towards the other. "Any word, if there's a problem with the mau—with the Koffre Institute for Earth Species Preservation, isn't that more important?" I took a scone, and after a moment Mossa did the same.

The requisite chewing delayed our conversation for a few minutes, which was probably a feature. The fire crackled, crumbs melted against my tongue, outside the gases furled and unfurled and the vast planet turned its swift rotation. At last Mossa, having ingested the entirety of her scone, picked up her tea cup, drank, and put it down again.

"A man has disappeared."

"Disappeared?"

"He was seen on a remote platform yesterday morning, and very thoroughly gone from it after an interval in which no railcars, communal or private, arrived or left."

"Radiation and recombinants!" I exclaimed, startled into the epithet. "Are you saying he threw himself into the planet?"

Mossa had taken advantage of my interjection to claim another scone and dust it with cinnamon, and she regarded me with raised eyebrow as she chewed her first bite.

"An exuberant verb you've chosen. But yes, the assumption is he stepped, leaped, or—"

"Was thrown off the platform," I said, putting down my own half-finished morsel. I remembered that she was here for a reason. "Did I know him?"

She shot her eyes at me again but, unsurprisingly, did not answer. Mossa would tell the story in her own way; it was part of her method. "He told someone on the platform, before he went over the edge, that he worked at Valdegeld." There was a speaking pause.

"Pleased with himself, was he?"

Mossa acknowledged this with an angled, noncommittal nod. "We checked for missing scholars here—he was old for a student—and got a description from those who saw him, on the platform and on the railcar he took to get there. We're fairly certain of his identity." A dismissive gesture. "Hardly difficult; there are very few eager to visit the platform whence he disappeared. But he didn't go there from Valdegeld. His journey had originated at the Preservation Institute."

I waited through her pensive silence, then said, "That seems a bit thin. You wouldn't have come to me based on that, so I suppose I know him."

Her eyes flicked at me, and I wondered what elaborate potential storylines had distracted her from my presence. "He arrived at the Preservation Institute directly from here," she said, brisk now. "He is employed at Valdegeld, in the Classics faculty; yes, I imagine you know him. Bolien Trewl."

My recollection of the melancholy reason for referring to him did not arrive in time to contain my habitual response to the name.

"Know him, and dislike him," Mossa stated.

I attempted a dismissive gesture, then gave up on it as a bad job. "Nobody likes him—I should say, none of my friends like him. He has his own crowd, I'm sure."

"I hope so," Mossa said mildly. "I would like to talk to them. But first tell me why you and others do not."

"Ugh, you know the type." I grinned at the impatient expression on her face, which said *I will, as soon as you tell me which it is.* "Self-important. Believes his own research is the most important consideration in any circumstance, except possibly his own comfort, preference, and conse-quence."

"But his research is important to him? Or only a means of making himself important?"

"Let me think. I've never wanted to spend this much time analyzing him before." I took another bite, chewed, swallowed, and drank some tea. "I think his research is vestigially important to him; that is, I think he chose his area because he believed in it, but by this point it's im-portant because *he* believes in it, rather than the other way around. And he is truly unbearable on the subject, far more than in other conversations, although he does like his own opinion about even the most trivial things." I tapped the plate between us. "The first time I met him, in my first week back here after—when I came back for the scholar post, he told me that the prickly pear scones were the best, I would be sure to like them the most, none of the others were worth trying." Years ago Mossa would have rolled her eyes in appreciation of this comemierdería with me, perhaps spouted some devastating critique; now she nodded distantly, understanding but not participating. I found myself deeply disliking her professionalism.

"What was his research area?" she asked.

I took another scone in compensation for emotional distress. "Altitude, he believed altitude explained everything there was to explain in organism distribution. Ugh, he could go on for hours. And I will say," I added around my crumbly bite, "that while he must have considered others and chosen it out of some reasoning, at this point it is all to his greater glory and I don't think he could hear the import of a word against it."

"What else?" Mossa asked. "You worked with him?"

"Thankfully, no. It would probably have happened at some point, but I've managed to stay on different projects. I did see him every once in a while. He was in another hall, but sometimes I would be there for dinner with a friend or I'd notice him at the table here. Or at the station, here or at the Preservation Institute—Tempests! I saw him five days ago!"

Mossa did not jerk upright, as I really thought she might have, just raised her eyelids a bit. "At the station?"

"In effect," I said, a bit disgruntled to be so drawn in. "And do you know, I thought at the time he looked a bit odd? But I was in a hurry, on my way back from the Institute, about to leave for the farm."

That got her at least shocked enough to pick up her cup of tea, and then put it down again and lift the pot to refresh us both. And her voice was sharp. "In what way odd?"

"Looked harried. I caught his eye—not on purpose!—and he turned away, wanted nothing to do with me. Oh stars, he was off to do something desperate, wasn't he?"

"Very probably," Mossa said. "But what?"

Chapter 2

Mossa submerged into her own calculations, playing out different storylines I supposed, focused and silent except for distracted slurps of tea. I refilled her cup once, and for a time lost myself in my own thoughts: a possible new configuration of the data from my current study; a film I had requested from the library for comparative purposes; how long Mossa might stay.

"Well." I stirred. "What will you do? Are you planning to stay here and speak with Bolien's friends, or are you going straight on to the Preservation Institute?"

Mossa's eyes were on the blue and yellow flames of the fire, but I felt observed nonetheless. "Would you be so good"—I glanced at her sharply; such stilted courtesy was unlike Mossa, at least in her dealings with me—"as to accompany me to speak with his friends and colleagues? I would undoubtedly miss the nuances of the academic community without your assistance," she added apologetically, as I glanced first at the inclement weather vibrating the window and then at my desk, laden with notes that I hoped to subsume into a data set, and that (someday!) into recommendations. "If you are not too overcome with work. I will buy you dinner, naturally. That way we can have a chance to catch up as well. I promised myself a meal at Slow Burn while I was here."

In truth, I could hardly have refused her; not only our desiccated friendship, but also the responsibility of assisting as I could with the inquiry into a colleague's sorry end—and a bit of curiosity forthwith—required it. I had even been telling myself that a chat with Bolien's colleagues might be useful for my work; while we were both in the Classics faculty, that prestigious discipline was enormous, with many subfields, committees, and convoluted relationships, and I could use a refresher on his area and their latest findings. Still, it cheered me disproportionately that Mossa was allocating time for a more leisurely conversation with me (even then, I did not imagine that said discussion would be work-free).

"Oh, very well," I said, hoping it sounded good-naturedly put-upon rather than ungracious. "Let me just look—" The university directory was on my desk, a hard laminate in the shape of the university's convoluted footprint itself, with notches for each of the buildings and overlay lenses that could flip on and off showing different types of data. I found Bolien's assigned laboratory. "Ah. Silahvet. Not *too* far from here." I glanced again at the window, but there was no help for it. "We can go ask whoever works near his desk and go on from there." I checked his supervisory committee while I was at it.

"Do you know anyone in the geography department?"

"Of course," I said, running through my acquaintances there in mind. "Perhaps—"

"Not Classical geography," Mossa interrupted. "Modern."

I stared. "*Modern* geography? Even Bolien's theories weren't that outlandish." I smiled at my own pun, but Mossa, usually enamored of such wordplay, was distracted.

"Perhaps it won't be necessary," she murmured.

"I daresay I can find someone if you want," I said doubtfully. "But you know as well as I do that the Classical and Modern sides don't mix much. I know more people in Speculative than in Modern."

"No matter." She swept her atmoscarf around her. "Shall we?"

The surface of Valdegeld platform was heated by the mechanisms at work below it, so at least the soles of our feet were warm as we fought through the freezing foggy gale. Even so, I was flustered and shivering by the time we reached Bolien's laboratory, well on the other side of Crickle Lane and halfway up the slope to the southern edge. We climbed the bridge over the 0°30' line, skirted the massive building that housed students belonging to Kofwanser College, and finally found the succor of Silahvet's looped entrance way.

Mossa looked around as we shook the fog from our wraps. "I don't think I ever came in here," she said.

"I doubt I did either, back then," I agreed, leading the way to Bolien's desk. "Strictly scholars or certified researchers, no classes. Not much reason for undergraduates to come through, unless you know one of the scholars, perhaps."

Now, as an appointed scholar myself, it was easy enough for me to identify and approach Bolien's colleagues. I havered a little at the first desk, not particularly wanting to give the reason for our questions, but Mossa slid easily into that role, explaining the situation dispassionately and calmly. I tried not to feel grateful; it was a great deal easier for her than it would have been for me, from both custom and inclination, as well as her lack of personal connection with the missing man.

It was made easier in that no one seemed to have known Bolien well, or liked him much. "The problem was," a food-chain scholar told us apologetically, "he *only* ever wanted to speak about work, and when he spoke about work he only wanted to talk about *his* work. He probably didn't see it that way, he probably thought he was having decent conversations with plenty of interdisciplinary information exchange, but he couldn't shut up about his own stuff and had no interest in anyone else's, and it showed."

All of this was as I had expected based on my few experiences with the man. There was however one piece of gossip that I hadn't been aware of: Bolien's desk-neighbor, a woman who specialized in the arctic ecosystem in the difficult pre-exploration era, claimed that Bolien had applied for my job. "Wouldn't have minded him moving, but I was still pleased when you got it instead," she said, nodding at me. Unable to find any appropriate words for that sentiment, I tweaked my fingers in a quick appreciation gesture.

"Sorry, I realize that's not what you were asking about . . ."

"On the contrary," Mossa replied. "Everything we can learn about his character is helpful."

The scholar looked at me in puzzlement and I tried to wave her concerns away; I was so familiar with my friend's approach that I had forgotten it could seem odd to other people.

Mossa continued. "What about colleagues? Anyone who worked with him particularly?"

"Not that I knew of. People *would* go to him when they had altitude questions, even if they grimaced about having to listen to the bluster. But he didn't have a particular mentor or patron, not that I ever heard."

"We've already heard in general about Trewl's research, but can you tell us of any recent developments? A specific problem he'd been working on lately, or something he was excited about?"

She considered, toying with a stylus. A parakeet on a wall perch above her desk chirped sleepily. "The last area I recall him talking about was the problem of 'sea level' and what that means over time." She shrugged. "Normally I filtered him out, but that has relevance for my research too. Not that he had anything groundbreaking to say about it. And I wouldn't say he was especially excited, either."

"Was he feeling low, lately? Depressed?"

"Oh no. Arrogant as ever. Can't really believe he would deprive all of us of his company, to be honest."

In that, everyone we spoke to concurred: Bolien had shown no signs of melancholy.

We emerged some time later from Incaster Lab, where we had been directed to find additional colleagues of the missing researcher, with no further information: he had been arrogant—not an unusual quality for a Classics scholar, and in between interviews I tried to tell Mossa I had indeed found some less obnoxious examples to be friends with since I myself was appointed—he had been enthusiastic about his research, and he had not shown any signs of despair.

"Any ideas about that Modern geographer?" Mossa asked, as we stood half-sheltered from the enormous wind, but at least isolated from anyone's hearing.

"But—" I stopped. I knew how Mossa worked; with an effort, I could follow her thinking. "You want to know why he went to that platform."

She nodded. "If he threw himself off, it's conceivable, though odd, that he would go to some symbolic and remote place like the easternmost platform. Although even in extremity that seems out of character for him. But if he did not plan to, and certainly nothing that we have heard makes him sound like a person in despair or agony . . ."

"Then why did he go to that platform?" I finished. "There was really nothing there?"

"Four residential buildings and a pub. With rather good food," she added dryly, "I suppose that's a possibility. But he didn't so much as have a conversation with anyone. At least beyond boasting of his affiliation with Valdegeld."

"Are you certain?"

She shrugged. "At the moment, I have no reason to disbelieve the people there. If we find anything that suggests they are lying, I will question them again. But . . ."

"Modern geographer, yes, I know." I squinted up at the swirling, motley clouds of the atmosphere. The perturbation was still too strong for me to make out even a blurry sun, but I knew it must be late. "It's near nightfall. Quick bite while I think?"

When humans first settled on Giant, they were horrified at the speedy rotation that would fit more than two complete day-night cycles into one of the sort they were used to, and arranged satellite mirrors to mimic the diurnal cycle on Earth. However, the mirrors proved overly complicated and inadequate for a number of reasons—it is far more disconcerting to have daylight flash on and off repeatedly due to a faulty joint rotator than to deal with a new schedule—and it turned out to be relatively easy for most people to adjust to being awake for a day and a night and then sleeping for a day and a night, even if it did sometimes lead to ennuis in aligning schedules. "You're fortunate I slept on the railcar," I added, starting towards my favorite of the nearby canteens.

Mossa did not reply directly, and I wondered whether she had found a way to check, during her investigation of Bolien Trewl, which diurnal cycle I was on. "Are your parents well?"

Again, I peered at her, unsure if this was a genuine query, a demonstration of her perspicacity, or an attempt to ascertain whether I was on visiting terms with someone else outside of Valdegeld. "How did you know I was there? How did you know to meet me at the station, come to that?"

Mossa hunched her shoulders. "Nothing terribly Investigatory. Your porter said you were away but expected back early today, and earlier you mentioned 'the farm.'"

"Oh. Did I?"

"I assumed only that of your parents would merit the definite article."

"Yes. Of course. And they are well enough, thank you. Working hard as always, although I convinced them to take a brief holiday off-platform while I was there." The satellite mirrors originally designed to replicate Earth's rhythms had been more usefully—urgently, even—repurposed to focus sunlight on crop cultivation platforms, like the one where I had grown up. And there was the rest of my answer, indeed: Mossa had guessed I was coming from my parents, had known I would be exhausted after helping them and readjusting to the heat and additional sunlight, and would certainly sleep as much as I could on the railcar journey.

Even as much as I could hadn't been much, however, and I confess to yawning a few times as we dined at my preferred canteen, The Stretch Goal, on bowls of the stew they kept simmering. Perhaps some of that was boredom, however. I was running through the Modern geography department in my mind, trying to decide whom to approach, but Mossa must have seen from my face that there was no one particularly appealing.

"If you think it best to send a message first," she said, dabbing at the dregs of her bowl with a doughy dumpling, "we could start with the Preservation Institute and return to talk to the Moderns."

"It might be better—wait. What do you mean *we*? I am not going to the mauzooleum tonight. I have a paper to finish."

Mossa has a number of different expressionless glares. She gave me one of them. "The Preservation Institute was the departure point for Bolien's trip. Especially since we have not found any evidence of a trigger for his disappearance here—"

"I understand," I said, impatiently. "But why do *I* need to go?"

"You have a unique perspective."

"Hardly unique. There are countless academics who make frequent use of the Institute . . ."

Mossa waved that aside. "But you also know *me,* and how I work. Explaining it to someone else would take too long."

I could not restrain a feeling of warmth as if that were praise or even affection and not merely a statement of fact.

Believing in signs of affection from Mossa was a trap, because it led to expecting signs of affection.

"I am sorry to postpone our dinner," Mossa went on, "but I believe we should proceed to the Preservation Institute as soon as possible."

I would have grumbled for the show of it, but I was not going to pretend that a meal, however delicious, was more important than investigating someone's disappearance, even someone I hadn't liked. "I suppose we can catch up on the railcar ride. As long as you invite me to Slow Burn another time," I added as I followed her outside, not wanting to lose that prospect entirely.

She turned towards me, cheek pressing against the winds, only her eyes visible through the atmoscarf. "You can go there any time. Or . . ."

I did not force her to ask about my finances, which were not overflowing but not in a state I could complain about. "I can't go there with *you* any time," I pointed out, and turned my attention back to fighting my way towards the appropriate station. "It has been a long time, Mossa."

"Indeed." After a pause, she went on. "If we leave directly for the Preservation Institute, we may not make it back before daybreak."

I shrugged. "The journey is short, and my rooms not far from the station. We can return late if necessary."

She waited a few steps before asking, "Is there somewhere we could stay there?"

"If it is necessary," I said, surprised. "But it seems easier to return and then go back the following day. Or perhaps I am simply inured to that railcar ride through custom." A thought occurred to me. "Do you have a place to sleep here?"

She turned back into the wind, head down. "The Investigators have rooms, or will cover the cost of one for the night, wherever I need to sleep."

Chapter 3

The railcar for the Koffre Institute for Earth Species Preservation left from the smallest of Valdegeld's three rail stations. The railcars were frequent, however, and we waited only a few minutes. The cabins were not particularly luxurious, but at that time of day there were few travelers and we had the long, rose velvet benches to ourselves.

"Well," I said, stretching my legs out till they almost reached her bench where it faced mine, an excusable indulgence since the heating pipes ran under the benches. "We have spent most of the day speaking to people who knew the man." I stopped, not wanting to say it.

"And nothing suggests he was in a mood to step into the crushing and freezing embrace of a gaseous abyss," Mossa finished.

I reached over and tweaked the knob on the grate, turning the fire up a little higher. "None of them liked him much."

Mossa tipped an eyebrow. "I nonetheless had the impression they would have noticed despondency ... although perhaps he was adept at hiding his moods ..."

"I meant, maybe that was a reason. Nobody liked him. If that made him melancholy, I don't think those are the people he would have told."

"True," Mossa said, tapping her knee, eyes on the swirling sea of fog outside the window.

"You don't seem convinced," I observed. "But what is the alternative? Someone on that isolated platform pushed him off?"

"Hmm."

"He was unlikeable, but he was only there for a few hours, right? Or is it possible he had some previous connection with someone there?"

"Perhaps. They might cover for one of their neighbors."

She said it neutrally, but I grimaced, certain our thoughts were running along similar lines. Sparsely populated platforms could be close-knit, and have little reason to help Investigators from denser parts of Giant's ring and platform network; if that was the case, getting one of them to tell the truth might be impossible. (And indeed, if Bolien Trewl had gone off somewhere and done something terrible to one of these people, made himself so unbearable that one of them had broken the anathema on breaching the edge of a platform, was it our affair to condemn them for that?) However, it was rare to find a small community so truly united. Imagining my parents' farming platform, which they shared with six other agricultural cultivators, I thought it more likely that petty spite bring a quick, if inconspicuous, denunciation.

"Could someone have followed him and hidden?"

"No one else disembarked from his railcar, and someone who arrived before him would almost certainly have been noticed. It really was a very scant place."

"Maybe he did jump, then," I said glumly, and we sat the rest of the journey in silence.

The Koffre Institute for Earth Species Preservation was established only shortly after Giant was settled by a geneticist named Krel Koffre. It was astonishing, now, to see it: platform after platform branching out from the conjunction of two rings that formed the station. Unlike most platforms on Giant, these were layered, steps leading up to new areas, so that you could get some sense of the scale from the railcar, even if you couldn't see how far it stretched to either side, which I knew was very far indeed.

There had, after all, been many species on Earth, once.

Even the small subset of that number whose genetic information had been collected before they were driven out of existence, and the far smaller fraction of those who had been resurrected for the mauzooleum, still resulted in an extremely large panoply of species. An extraordinary amount of space had been dedicated to recreating their habitats in this entirely hostile environment.

It was an almost unthinkable extravagance on a planet where there was no land that had not been constructed. Agricultural and residential space were still considered dreadfully scarce. But the mauzooleum had been created in a post-traumatic moment. Koffre had been a part of the biopreservationist movement at the end of the world and used their moral and scientific legitimacy to argue that keeping the species of Earth in their potential form in seed banks and on data caches was not enough: that as many examples as possible should be gestated into living plants and animals. Moreover, during the initial settlement scientists—biological and social—were deeply, almost hysterically concerned about the consequences of living on a planet with no other life larger than microbes; gestating Earth species was considered a necessity for humans. Now, with cats and cockroaches infesting almost every platform, the extravagant facilities developed to address that concern seemed laughable, but the administrators of the Preservation Institute had guarded its historic privilege jealously, and their links with Valdegeld helped protect it as well. How, after all, would Earth ever be restored if the animals and plants could not be reconstituted, or could not be cared for once they were? How could the project of restoration and reseeding, the entire purpose of the vaunted field of Classical studies, be understood without access to this living resource? And many non-scholars visited as well, finding some importance in seeing for themselves these creatures and plants, even if they were not, quite, in their native habitat; a respite perhaps, or a warped window on what our lost life on Earth might have been like.

I had visited often enough for my work that I had my routine of where to look on the approach. Out the right side of the car and up to the midlevel platform, where if I was lucky I would catch the wide stripes of a zebra. The feeding trough for the mammoths just beyond that. Then to the left, where a field of wildflowers bordered the rail. Just beyond them the jaguar could sometimes be spotted if it chose to lounge near the edge of its habitat. Back to the right for the giant tortoise. And, almost invisible at the very upper limit of the window, a dark blur that I knew to be a vat of fantastically rare and expensive soil, literal Earth, populated with worms.

There were of course animal rights activists who argued that the animals shouldn't have been reconstituted to live in what was, essentially, captivity. This perspective had not picked up many adherents; probably, I always thought, because many of the species in the mauzooleum had more space to wander around in than most human residential platforms offered. If they were in captivity on this inhospitable planet, then so were we.

Chapter 4

The Preservation Institute station was lined with hotels for the many tourists, as well as the scholars from Valdegeld and from farther afield, who came to witness the organisms. People were not allowed into the habitat platforms, but a network of walkways offered several different paths for observation. These could be a bit unscientific—the *Cute Animals Promenade*, for example, did not include every animal *I* would consider cute—but the popular appeal helped the mauzooleum to stave off the pressure to give up their platform space for *human* residence, as did the more distant platforms within the cluster dedicated to experimental agriculture and animal husbandry.

I led Mossa away from the path entrances, towards the administrative buildings sited unobtrusively behind the hotels. "I'm not sure whom Bolien usually worked with," I warned her. "We may need to ask around before we find someone who can tell us exactly what he was doing here that day."

Mossa nodded impassively. "Lead on."

We started with my usual contact, a mousy man who blinked a lot and was both knowledgeable and helpful on my subjects. He frowned when I mentioned Bolien. "I never worked with him myself," he said, "but the name does sound familiar. I don't suppose you have a picture?"

Mossa flipped open her notebook and configured the page to show a snap of Bolien. From where I was sitting the pattern of light and dark didn't quite resolve, but the shape of it nevertheless called to mind his faculty visual, familiar from any number of university informationals. I shivered, briefly overtaken by the awfulness of this task.

"I've certainly seen him around. Ah, yes, I think I remember who he works with . . . give me a moment."

When my colleague returned he brought with him a beaky woman, taller than I or even Mossa and dressed in a fire-blue coat I instantly coveted. Mossa, appearing unmoved by her sartorial panache, asked about Bolien. "Have you worked with him long?"

The woman, whose name was Cyla, told us she had been meeting with him for years, but only occasionally. "It would be a stretch to say we worked *together*, really," she said, her gaze sliding from Mossa's face to mine and back. "He wanted me to give him access to whatever habitat he was aiming for that day. He was not particularly interested in, for example, my opinions, or my expertise."

Mossa flicked a glance at me. "That's not how it usually works?"

I shook my head as Cyla smiled. "Most people, especially from the university"—she gave me a nod, but her attention was fixed on Mossa—"want to discuss with us. They check their theories against what we've observed of the animals in their habitat. We have some zones of species interaction; sometimes they petition for a specific combination to be introduced, or want to do observation of a particular time—feeding, for example, or a simulation of a certain season."

I suspected that Mossa's question had included an additional uncertainty. "Outsiders can't visit the habitats without someone from the Institute accompanying them. Even for accredited scholars, Preservation Institute staff will always be on hand, at least unless there's quite a large degree of trust. Beyond the tourist paths, that is, but those are limited and don't get very close to the animals or to any plants that aren't commonly grown on Giant."

Mossa nodded. "I suppose that's for security."

"Our security," Cyla said, "their safety. And our reputation."

"Hm?"

"We are under a great deal of pressure because of the amount of living space and other resources that we use. There has been proposal after proposal to appropriate some or all of our platforms, either in situ or removing them to another convergence. The tourism helps quite a bit—that is, in fact, the only reason we have the paths. But suggestions of lax security on the one hand, or accusations of blocking off access to legitimate researchers on the other, have both been used against us at various times." She spread her hands. "It's a narrow rail."

Mossa tilted her head. "I would have thought that the safeguarding of all these species was reason enough?"

"The species are safeguarded through the biological samples, kept in the vault as well as, for most of them, in other more dispersed places; and backup copies of the genome maps, which are in a number of servers and data caches all over Giant. Gestating living examples is, according to some"—Cyla elongated her expression—"a luxury."

"Indeed," Mossa murmured, managing to hit the same tone of mild irony. She waited a beat to shift the subject. "When was the last time you saw Bolien?"

Cyla flipped open a scheduler. "A few weeks ago, I think . . . Ah, here: thirty-eight local days ago. He wanted to see the rock pool environment we've been working on. Spent a full day there, and part of the night as well."

"You didn't see him six or seven days ago? Local days."

"No . . ." Cyla hesitated, scattered her scheduler images again. "No, I didn't have a meeting with him."

"Is there any way to find out whom he did meet?"

"I can send a bulletin to everyone and see who answers. It may take a day or two to get a response."

Mossa tap-transferred her contact information. "If you could let me know."

"Of course."

It was well past midnight when we left the meeting. I was weary, my sleep on the railcar from my parents' not having been very restful, and Mossa must have been too—I hadn't even asked which diurnal she was on—and yet it seemed a shame to drag her back to Valdegeld so quickly. "Have you ever been here?" I asked. "We could walk one of the tourist paths before we return, if you like."

Mossa acquiesced willingly enough—odd for her, she was usually single-minded to a fault—and I chose one of the shorter circuits in deference to our long day of working.

It had been some time—years, I realized—since I had walked around the mauzooleum without some specific purpose and destination in mind, and despite my familiarity with the environment I still found it impressive. The paths we walked, made of the same coated and reinforced metal as all platforms, had been carved or pressed with the images of various Classical organisms, or of the traces they might leave, creating the illusion of fossils in the ground or footprints leading to a watering hole; the illusion that there was some ingrained history of life on this planet. Lamps guttered bluely at intervals, leaving the pathway dim, but the habitats—all some little distance away, and protected by transparent walls—glowed brightly with an approximation of what sunlight would look like on Earth.

I found the walk and the unaccustomed images helped to clear my head—perhaps that was Mossa's reasoning. But odd that Mossa should think that way—

She didn't. Of course she didn't.

"You think something important happened here," I said suddenly, breaking our ruminative silence. "To Bolien, before he left. You think his time here was decisive."

"It seems likely," Mossa responded, "but I am far from certain. You did mention he looked unusual when you saw him at the station before he came here." I nodded, wondering if I had been correct or was recording over my memory in light of what I now knew. "In any case, it deserves an hour for getting a better sense of this place. I will say," she added, looking down the deliberately twisting path ahead of us, "he certainly does not seem the type to wander aimlessly around a place which he visits frequently."

"Unless he was truly distraught?" I suggested, but when Mossa turned her skeptical glance on me I held up my hands immediately. "No, I agree. He must have come here for a reason. I hope we may find out soon whom he met with, what they spoke of."

"Indeed," Mossa replied, and I cast her a sharp look, unconvinced by her tone, but dimness had overtaken us, and I couldn't read her expression. "It is late," she added, turning her face briefly to the dragonfly enclosure, its walls pocked with magnifiers. "Shall we return?"

"Yes," I agreed with a sigh. Cyla would contact us if anyone responded, and there seemed no reason to remain at the Institute to wait. "Er . . ." It would be awkward whether I offered her a place to stay or didn't. I attempted, therefore, to determine which outcome I would prefer.

Normally, I enjoy my solitude. In particular, I was still enamored of my scholar's rooms, so much more comfortable than the very tolerable space I had enjoyed at Valdegeld as a student. I savored my every arrival in them, closed the door behind me with a sense of sufficiency and safe enclosure. There was a small guest room with a narrow bed attached, and while I gloried in the idea of inviting someone—in student days we had to reserve the shared guest room of the hall, or content ourselves with blankets on the floor—I had not yet had occasion to do so, and my rooms felt inviolate.

And yet. Though my eyes sagged with weariness, the thought of spending this evening alone chimed incomplete. It must be, I told myself, the allure of the mystery. Surely Mossa had some additional reflections that she might share in the ease of an overnight?

And in any case, *Mossa* hardly counted as a guest.

"You'll stay at mine, of course," I said therefore, as jovially as I could manage, as we turned back towards the station. The assumption of normalcy was, I thought, my best strategy. I remembered also I should clarify the situation. "As a scholar, I have space for a guest—only a closet, really, but you'll be quite comfortable. And you still owe me that meal."

Mossa grunted. "As soon as we can manage it without events overtaking us," she said, and I had turned to ask whether she expected *events* to occur soon and of what sort when a blur sprang through the air, slamming her to the hard metal of the platform. I found myself breathless, but managed to topple towards her, screaming or gasping in some combination of alarm and anger. There were, I remembered as I staggered forward, emergency buttons studded on the railings along the walkways; my fingers found the hard edge of one and swept across it as I directed a kick, poorly aimed and worse balanced, at the vibrating clutch of muscle and pelt that crouched on Mossa's curled body. The animal hissed at me, but my boots were heavy ones and it was at least distracted enough to focus its eyes and its claws towards me. I kicked again, swiped my sleeve-wrapped arm in its general direction in an attempt to frighten it. I was still bellowing for assistance, but I couldn't imagine anyone coming. I bethought myself of another weapon, and snatched an ignition from my pocket. In the platform's oxygenated atmosphere, it created only a small spark, but I waved it as close to the beast as I dared, hoping to trigger some epigenetic fear of flame.

It bared its glistening sharp teeth at me—some sort of feline, my Classically trained brain informed me—and then, quick as lightning, it whipped back to look over its shoulder, and sprang into the night.

I collapsed to the platform, choking with residual shock, before I could stop myself, and dragged myself to Mossa's side without coming upright. To my relief, she was already rolling, and in a moment I saw her face, draped in her atmoscarf and apparently unscathed.

I found I was running my hands over her shoulders and arms—to assure myself that she was unharmed, most naturally—and I stopped myself at once. "You're well?"

Mossa was uncurling herself and managed a sitting position. "Unharmed, and very grateful that this facility apparently keeps their caracals well-fed. And to you, of course." The afterthought was so typical of Mossa—and, if I was fair, in this case so accurate—that I barely felt its sting. "I take it that's not a usual occurrence?"

I laughed, felt the giggles of released tension on its edge and stopped quickly. "Hardly! You're really unhurt? Can you stand?"

I helped her to her feet, and held her arm as we started back towards the station. I kept glancing around for a swift-moving shadow, and she repeated her question.

"No," I said more clearly, "I have never heard of an animal getting loose here. Although . . ."

"Hmm?" She had not disengaged her arm, but she wasn't leaning on me either, or at least not much.

I looked around again. "I suppose it's not the sort of thing they would want people to know about."

"Certainly not."

When we reached the station, I wanted to settle Mossa in the waiting railcar while I informed the staff about the escape, but she wouldn't hear of it and so we both went into the administrative building and told the first person we found. It was a little difficult to extricate ourselves, what with their anxiousness to confirm that we wouldn't spread the event all over the rings, but we managed to board the railcar just before it left.

"Altogether, a very instructive visit," Mossa said. She was sitting very straight on the cushioned bench, as though to deny any hint of tiredness, but she had to be exhausted.

"We'll go straight to my rooms and order something to eat there," I said encouragingly. "You can bathe while we're waiting for the food, and then sleep." I shook my head, the horror of the feline's sudden attack striking me again. "Mossa . . . of all the things to happen . . ."

"Not so surprising, really, given the setting."

"*Very* surprising. I still can't believe you weren't injured."

"It wasn't hunting. It was startled."

"Startled by what?"

She didn't answer.

Chapter 5

When we got back to Valdegeld it was close to dawn. The streets were not empty; at any given time the population would be staggered across sleep patterns. But few people were about; it was nearing the end of a diurnal, when those who had been awake were preparing for bed, and moreover the weather was still intemperate, with strong gusts plowing along the platform.

We staggered along through the gales, thick clouds obscuring most of the moon-spotted sky, gas lights flickering with the atmosphere gaps that the wind introduced into the aged piping. I was so tired—the depletion of adrenaline, I diagnosed—that I was counting each step, trying to trick myself into believing the distance to my rooms was shorter than it was. As we neared the corner of Zaybel Road, however, Mossa paused. "I see Rechaure is still in his usual spot."

I glanced at her curiously, both because I hadn't realized she was on named terms with the fanatic, and because her voice sounded worryingly distant, as though even she were coming to the ends of her endurance. "Yes," I said, "he's generally at that corner."

The end-of-the-world preacher, for such was the person she had indicated, usually stood on the street accosting passersby with his version of history. At this time of night, though, he was silent, wrapped in atmosblankets and slumped against the wall. By the pile of fabric that presumably sheltered him a small angled sign, weighted against the wind, proclaimed his views for him: *WE DESERVE THIS LIFELESS PLANET* on one side, *WE ARE ALL COMPLICIT IN THE APOC-ALYPSE* on the other. "Strange for him to be out in this weather," Mossa said.

I tried to remember whether I had seen him during previous storms, but by then we were past the corner and my attention shifted to getting us to my rooms. By the time we reached the stairs Mossa had slowed significantly, and I restrained my longing for the warm fire, knowing she would not thank me for hurrying her, commiserating, or even noticing her difficulty. Indeed, I kept my eyes turned away as I matched her pace on the three flights, and it was not until I had finally shut my door on that inclement night, ignited the fire, and turned back to her that I saw the blood on her jacket.

"Mossa!" Before I knew it I was beside her and grasping her shoulders; she had tried to shift the snitching stains away from my view. She ceased resisting and I rotated her gently towards me so that I could examine the several splotches of blood along her back.

"It didn't maul me," she said, in the tone of someone determined to clarify some point of importance in the face of utter exhaustion. "It just"—she curled her fingers demonstratively—"grabbed."

"Why didn't you say something sooner, you absolute buffer?" I expostulated. "Never mind. Go bathe, that's the thing to start—warm water, and then we'll see if we need to send for the medic." She obediently started towards the bathroom. "Do you need—er, do you need help removing your shirt?"

She hesitated only a moment. "I think I can manage."

I nodded, stifling an unworthy disappointment. Mossa took two more steps on the soft carpet and then stopped again. "It occurs to me that I may not be able to adequately clean the wounds."

I nodded once more, then realized she wasn't looking at me. "Call when you're ready."

The bathroom—how grateful I was to have a private bathroom, and a deep tub—was off the short hall between the parlor, my bedroom, and the guest room, so I didn't see her enter it, although the suggestion of a gasp marked the moment when she removed her shirt. She had left the door of the bathroom open, and I could hear the click of the gas jet heating the water, then the rush as it poured into the tub.

They say our ancestors in those final days on Earth had no heated water for washing, certainly not enough to fill a tub, with their every resource thrown towards the final desperate twin tasks of escaping the planet they had destroyed and making another one livable. I've always been skeptical of that story; I'm sure there were people who believed that their *own* indulgence wouldn't matter in the larger scheme of scarcity. But it was doubtless true for many people, and I pitied them thoroughly as I rose in response to Mossa's call, and stepped into the dim-lit bathroom. They never would have seen a sight like this: the arch of her warm back lapsing from the water, muscles and spine curved in harmony on a theme. I guess some sound escaped me at the sight of the clotted punctures in her smooth skin, for Mossa said, in something quite nearly identical to her usual tone, "Come now, it's not so bad. But I do believe that a thorough cleanse is a sensible idea." She reached the soap back to me with a graceful arm.

There was a slight ooze to the wounds, I found, probably from when she had removed her shirt. I thought with a shudder of how stiffly she had sat in the railcar on the way back. "Why didn't you say something earlier?" I murmured again.

"What would we have done differently?" Her voice was flat; naturally, she had thought it through. "I was not ready to have my wounds treated there, nor to spend the night."

My eyes, my whole focus still on her skin, I grasped for some possible answer. "We could have gotten a stasis pill from the Institute clinic, or," since that seemed excessive even to me, "an analgesic, gotten you back here without the pain."

Mossa snorted and then hissed as the motion jerked the wounds. "It's hardly worth the fuss," she replied, scoffing but so softly.

My fingers danced just over the aligned claw points: five each in two places near her shoulders, and as she leaned further still, four on either side near her hips. I frothed the soap into bubbles, slid as softly as I could. I did not linger unnecessarily, I refused to, though necessity was a blurry and disputed concept, I thought, watching my fingers slip the bubbles across her skin. "We'll need to apply some disinfection podules," I told her, my voice commendably even. I was drenched in the intensity of the sensations. Attempting to concentrate my mind on anything else, I found myself striking on something she had said earlier, which I had not paid enough attention to at the time: she hadn't wanted to spend the night at the Institute, though doing so had been her idea; and, even before, that the beast had been startled, not hunting. "You suspect someone set the feline on you deliberately?"

Mossa shrugged, her muscles shifting under my fingertips, my tender palm. "As you suggested, I can't imagine it happens often that an animal gets loose, certainly not the larger, more dangerous ones. There are too many casual visitors for that to be viable."

"We decided to walk there on a whim," I said slowly, working it out.

"But there must be cameras," Mossa countered. "At the station and the entrance to the paths if nowhere else."

"Someone within the Preservation Institute, then?" I asked in dismay.

"It could have been a physical watcher as well. We made no secret of our departure or our destination; if someone was waiting outside the offices they would have seen us start on the paths. Although," she added, and, as my hands released her back, stood and reached for a towel, "I imagine it would be more difficult for someone not closely related to the Institute to release an animal."

"Not to mention guide it towards its target," I agreed. "Although I think I will look up the Classical zoologists studying cats of that type, to be thorough."

"A fine idea." She turned towards me, swathed in the soft material, and I saw the exhaustion in her features.

"We'll be better off after some rest," I told her. "And food! What would you like?"

She made a gesture of disinterest, but I remembered when she had been ill or tired at university she had favored soup, and the laksa in this hall was particularly good. I ordered two bowls, placed the disinfection podules without letting my fingertips touch her skin, lent her a robe, and chatted incessantly in an attempt to keep her awake until the food arrived. She only managed to finish half of her bowl before mumbling something and retiring to her room. I stayed awake a bit longer, staring out at the wind-torn tendrils of gas and moisture that draped the night and pondering.

Chapter 6

I intended to let Mossa sleep in the morning, had plans in fact of ordering up those scones again—for I remembered her tendency towards baked goods at breakfast—as an anticipation of her wants. A treat. But when I edged quietly from my bedroom in my dressing gown, she was already pacing the parlor, dressed and fidgety.

"I'm concerned," she said, as I emerged from the hall.

"So I see," I said, trying not to be short. "Breakfast?"

She made a dismissive gesture and I put in the order for the scones anyway. I remembered this mood of hers from when we were students (and did very well on far less sleep and food); scones at least were more or less portable, if she was about to hare off somewhere.

"If we're assuming that someone at the Preservation Institute set the cat on us"—I noted the *us*—"then the request for information about Bolien is only likely to alarm that person more, draw more attention." She continued pacing. The fire was burning, but low, and I went over to turn it up a fraction against the chill in the air. "I should have done something about it yesterday, I should have—" She clenched her fist.

"A cat," I said, releasing some of my insights from the previous night, "however vicious and clawed, is hardly a robust means of assassination."

Mossa stopped and whirled on me. "Exactly! It was an opportunist move, perhaps a warning. But what happens next . . ."

Yes, I knew this mood. Distraction was the only approach I had found that worked. "What were you planning for today?"

Unexpectedly, she cracked a grin. "Slow Burn, hopefully."

"Oh yes," I agreed, and our smiles met and locked into that utter understanding we had once shared. When the bell rang for the dumbwaiter I didn't even mind, and went smiling to open the cupboard.

"Ah, brilliant idea, Pleiti," Mossa said in delight when she saw the plate. "I must be hungry if I'm already thinking about our dinner. But to answer your question more seriously." She took a scone, doused it with powdered sugar, then carefully grasped around the dusting and bit and chewed before continuing in a more sober tone. "On reflection, I'm afraid we may have to put off our dinner again after all. I believe it's increasingly urgent for me to return to the platform he disappeared from. Although I would like to try to talk to a Modern geographer before going back there."

I nodded, taking my own scone. "I had a look at the directory last night. I have some ideas of whom to contact. We can arrange a meeting, or three, as soon as you like."

It occurred to me, through the flush of being helpful and capable, that if Mossa went back to that platform she was as likely as not to find the solution to the mystery there, and have no reason to return. We might be putting our dinner off until the next time she had a case that tangentially involved my profession.

The same thought must have struck her, almost certainly long before I thought of it. "Pleiti," she began, in the cautious tones of someone about to say something with unpredictable effects, and then there was a knock on the door.

I felt my lips forming an unnecessary apologetic smile as I dragged my gaze away from Mossa's and went to the door.

On the landing stood one of the porters, Brez. Like all the porters he was an aged rail worker, given what is considered a sinecure in respect for his age and experience, but in this conception of an easy job they didn't consider the three flights of steps in gravity a little heavier than what his muscles had evolved for, and he was leaning against the wall panting slightly.

"Are you all right? Will you come in and sit down? Cup of tea?" I expected him to hand me a paper slip of a message before possibly accepting or otherwise shaking his head and trudging back down again, but instead he straightened.

"People to see you. Investigators."

"Investigators," I repeated stupidly. "I have an Investigator visiting me at the moment."

"Yes, they're actually hoping to see her, I think."

The Investigators had remained in the porter's lodge, which at least seemed to indicate we weren't wanted for the disappearance of a unique animal from the mauzooleum, so we went down to see them there.

The weather had worsened, moisture-bearing gales whipping red and orange and pallid fogs through the atmosphere beyond the windows, and the fire in the porter's lodge was turned up high. The Investigators—two of them, one square-set and large-eyed, the other narrower and more rounded—were settled in the chairs by the fire and looked disinclined to move. I didn't blame them: those chairs had heating tubes through their frames and were beyond lovely on a cold day. Nonetheless, they rose—the smaller one first—to greet us and hovered until I urged them back to their seats.

"What is it?" Mossa asked. I would have wondered if she knew them, to be so direct and informal, but she might have been that way with anyone, and especially in the mood she was in already.

"We were hoping you could help us out, in fact, Senior Investigator," said the larger one, with an element of humility in his voice. I managed not to send a surprised look at my friend: I had not at all realized she was so advanced, so well respected, in her profession. Not that I was surprised she excelled, anyone could have known that; only that it was so readily recognized.

"What happened?" Mossa asked, with an edge to her voice that said she was repeating herself, or near enough.

"We found a body," answered the smaller one, her eyes deep-set and long-lashed. "Not in very good shape, given the—" She gestured at the storm outside. "But we're pretty sure he was helped to his end."

"Here?" I asked precipitously, and they turned their level gazes to me without haste, but Mossa touched my hand.

"Not Bolien," she said quietly. "Rechaure."

That *did* startle the Investigators, nearly as much as it surprised me. "Begging your pardon, Senior Investigator," the larger one said, "and I'm sure it's your business to know everything, but *how did you know*?"

"We saw his post last night—not him, he wasn't visible, but his blankets and his sign shouldn't have been out there on a night like that. He always used to go to the hostel on Blinkstart when the tempests got strong. I should have known, I should have *looked* last night."

I opened my mouth to remind her that she had been hurt, but even in her self-recrimination she was aware enough to direct a warning glance my way, and I shut it again. I felt a foolish knot of heat coalesce inside me at the thought of her weakness, a secret between us; but of course she had tried to keep it from me as well. I only knew because she couldn't hide it any longer.

"Where did you find the body?" Mossa went on, sharper now. The Investigators exchanged glances again and she made a sharp, dismissive motion. "If you had found it in his blankets, at his usual spot, it would have taken longer than this to determine that it was not caused by the storm."

"Accurate," the deep-eyed smaller one replied with a sigh. "The body was found at the rail station."

"Which one?" Mossa snapped out, almost before she finished.

"The main station," the Investigator replied, sounding slightly surprised by her vehemence. "He was in the waiting room, laid out on one of the benches. Skull fracture."

"Blood?"

"Not enough for it to have happened on the bench."

Mossa nodded slowly. "Well." She turned to me. "So

sorry, my dear Pleiti, but it seems I'll have to take a look at this. On balance, though, I doubt I'll be traveling tonight. Maybe you could make the dinner reservations? I hope you can manage to finish that research you were telling me about; you can fill me in when we meet."

Chapter 7

I wished my rooms had gas-heated chairs.

I wished I had a consequential job that required my immediate attention.

No, that wasn't fair. There was nothing more consequential than my job, which was a necessary, a crucial step in reclaiming Earth. But I was only a tiny molecule in that immense effort, whereas Mossa seemed irreplaceably central to her tasks.

The tempest raged beyond my windows, driving dust and torn clouds through the wind-alleys between the buildings. Better to be inside than out. But Mossa wouldn't be outdoors, would she? No clues for even so honed an eye as hers, surely, not in this weather. She would be dry, if not warm, at the morgue (where was the morgue in Valdegeld? At the hospital perhaps? Or the Investigators Bureau?); or maybe at the station, where he had been found. It would be drafty there, with the big gaps at each end for the railcars to pass through, and cold even in the waiting room where Rechaure had been found.

Why would anyone kill Rechaure? He had been a fixture in Valdegeld since our student days, since before then. There were whispers that he had been a scholar himself, perhaps even a Don, before some academic or moral failing had seen him cast out, forced to haunt his beloved university from the streets that ran through it. Others told that he had abandoned the academy of his own volition, furious or vainglorious or claiming some ethical high ground that would not permit him to continue to associate himself, and pushed him instead to rant at all comers about the end of the world. I didn't even know if the end of the world was his expertise, or if he had been a history scholar at all. Perhaps he had never been associated with the university; perhaps he came from one of the many shops and families that sustained the school and its population, or perhaps he had arrived one day from elsewhere and seen the opportunity to yell at over-indulged young people and slightly less indulged older people.

But he had always been there, he always said the same things. Why would anyone see the need to kill him now?

My eyes strayed again to the window. I had my work in front of me: my text, my map overlays, my numbers, and pinned to the back of my workspace pictures of every animal and plant represented in this particular history. But I looked again and again at the window, though I could see little there but streamers of pale and glowing fog.

I threw down my interface after some time, and rose to pace around the room. Mossa had, at least, suggested she would return, although it was too easy for me to imagine her, dogged and intense, on the trail of some clue. But she had said—she had said, in fact, that I was to make the dinner reservation. Glancing at the clock, I caught up my jacket—even the stairwell required it, on such a day—and trundled back down to the porter's rooms again.

Such wireless transmissions as existed on Earth are impossible in this dense atmosphere, and most inter-platform communication is by hand-delivered message. There were some telegraph lines laid along the rails, particularly on the major rings, but they weren't very reliable in the corrosive atmosphere and the blustering, violent weather. However, on large platforms like Valdegeld there were often telephone lines, most cached underground between the streets and the platforms proper, and in my hall there was an instrument outside the porter's rooms. I had to wait while Lessenan, a scholar in Classical chemistry with a one-eyed cat and a taste for loud music, finished a conversation—a shouted conversation, although from what I could hear it didn't sound angry, so it was the wind or her own frayed timpani that caused the yelling.

Waiting, I checked the bulletin board by the telephone compartment. When I had perused all the general announcements—a benefaction of used books, slightly tarnished, to firstcomers; the dean of the Moderns announcing a festival *celebrating our unique Gigantesque way of life,* which I automatically read in the snidely resentful tones of one whose department was always an afterthought; the menu in the hall kitchen for the next week—I added the overlay for the Classics department. The dean (doubtless encouraged by the rector) had posted a notice about the new formalities for reserving computational power, which I had already read and diagnosed as unnecessary but which were nonetheless mandated; the University rector (doubtless encouraged by

the dean) had deigned to praise a recent monograph out-
lining the partial biological map of the Tasmanian Island,
1912–1920; and the Classics canteen (possibly encouraged
by the previous two notices) was offering a special two-for-
one on fermented drinks.

"Oh, hullo Pleiti," Lessenan boomed, coming out of the
booth. "How've you been? Seen anything good lately?"

We were both aficionados of Valdegeld's amateur dra-
matics scene, and the professional opera when we could
afford it, and occasionally joined together for a show. It was
very pleasant, and I liked Lessenan, but at that moment I
felt frantic to avoid any entanglement that might make me
miss time with Mossa during her undoubtedly brief (if it
was not already over) visit.

"Nothing much," I said, as cheerfully as I could manage.
"See you at the chorale on Marsday?" And I ducked past
her into the booth before she could so much as answer.

I was able to connect with Slow Burn without too much
difficulty, and they still had tables available for late that
night. I replaced the receiver, but I was reluctant to return
to my empty room and continue my research. What had
Mossa said? *Finish that research you were telling me about*—
but I hadn't told her about any of my research, not specif-
ically, and certainly not any piece small enough to finish.

I snapped my fingers and raced up the stairs to my room
again to flip through my university directory: Modern geography. She had been asking for my help; yes, she had
been dragged off to deal with this new incident, since the
local Investigators thought so highly of her, but *naturally*
she didn't want to let go of Bolien's case. I penned a few
notes to what I thought were the most likely possibilities,
then hurried back downstairs again—at least I was getting

my exercise, storm notwithstanding—to tap on the porter's door. It was still Brez's shift, and I looked at him doubtfully as I handed over my sheaf of messages. "I hate to ask you to go out in this fearful weather," I started, wondering if I should attempt to telephone instead, but trying to catch someone in their rooms or offices was always dubious.

He chuckled at me. "Not to worry! Plenty of people going to and from, even in this miserable storm. You know well enough, if we stopped every time there was a blow we wouldn't get anywhere. I'll find someone who has to go in the right direction, never fear."

I thanked him and returned to my rooms. They seemed far cozier, and my calculations far more promising, once I had done something for Mossa's investigation as well.

_ _ _ _ _ _ _

Chapter 8

Mossa returned some hours later, a gust of energy blowing into the room as though driven by the storm.

"Well," she said, "well, well, well. I was sorry to leave you all day, Pleiti, but needs must." She looked tired, and I guessed from the pattern of her face that the wounds in her back were paining her, had been wearing away at her for some time, and yet she was also undoubtedly pleased with herself, and that sustained her like nothing else. "Were you able to do as I asked?"

"Naturally you had to go to work, Mossa," I said. "Think nothing of it. And yes, the reservation is in—oh, just over an hour. Time for you to rest up a bit."

She did not want to rest, of course. "And the other? Did you—?"

"A Modern geographer?" I waited for her to nod, her eyes glowing. "Three possibilities, available for us to visit tomorrow. I'll go through their qualifications with you, you can select which one. But for now, let me check your bandages, since I don't suppose you've had a doctor look at your back."

Mossa shook me away. "It's fine, I'm fine, but do you mind ringing for tea? It's been a chilly day!" She rubbed her hands together by the blue flame of the fire, practically cackling.

"You'll tell me about it, I hope," I said, with very little hope that she wouldn't. I wanted to know, of course, and wanted to hear it from her even more, but most of all I wanted her to take care of those vicious scratches on her back and maybe sit down or have a drink, or do whatever might relax the tension from her shoulders. It seemed that was tea, so I obediently put in the order, with the addition of some biscuits.

She was already overflowing with words. ". . . condition of the body, naturally, not what one could have wished . . ." I fetched a washcloth, and, with a gesture of distracted acquiescence, she lifted the back of her shirt for me while she talked. ". . . moisture, and no one knows exactly how long it was there unattended, although I suspect—"

At that interesting juncture we were interrupted, for the second time that day, by a knock on the door. I exhaled in pointed annoyance; I wasn't sure I'd be able to get her to let me look at her injuries so easily again. At least my quick appraisal had shown that there hadn't been much, if any, fresh bleeding, and no obvious infection around the bandages. I let her tuck her shirt back in and went to open the door.

The porter stood there—not Brez, he would be off now; it was the scrawny one who had started recently and usually worked when I slept, so I hadn't learned his name yet, but worse still there was a man behind him, a stout man with an expansive bearing. Porters weren't supposed to allow anyone up until we had agreed to it, although given the stairs they did sometimes bend that rule.

"Yes?" I iced.

The porter shuffled slightly. "Beg pardon. He said you requested a meeting with him."

I let my eyes track up to meet the other man's, and he stepped forward immediately with his heavy hand out in greeting. "Viken Porbal, of the Modern geography department. You sent me a note, and as I happened to be passing . . ."

I was still attempting to resign myself to touching his hand when Mossa appeared by my side, coat on. "Oh indeed! Professor Porbal. How kind of you to come to us. Perhaps we could speak in the common room," she added, not quite a question, turning her intensity on the porter, who wilted.

"It's, err. . . ." he began. "I believe, that, err. . . ."

"In use?" I asked briskly, taking up the cue. "Well. The games room then, or the library. We'll find a quiet spot." I let Mossa slide past me and locked the door, and we followed the apologetic porter on a tour of the public spaces of my rather narrow dormitory.

The library wasn't completely empty, but Mossa exclaimed genially that we weren't discussing anything so very private, in any case, and took a seat at a table in an unoccupied corner, and I sat down immediately beside her, so Porbal had little choice but to settle himself across from us.

"I'm sorry if I intruded," he said, his eyes flicking between us. "An awkward time of day, perhaps, but as I was passing . . . but then, if you prefer we could meet tomorrow instead."

"Oh no, no," Mossa responded, full of good cheer, "I did want to get this information as soon as possible, I'm quite pleased you stopped by, very kind of you indeed."

He hrumphed a bit, as if not entirely sure whether to take her at face value (*I* certainly wouldn't have), and then recovered his enthusiasm. "What can I help you with?"

Mossa pulled a railcar map—*my* railcar map, I noticed—from the pocket of her coat. "We have reason to believe someone stepped off the platform at this station," she said, fingertip on the slightly raised point at the northeastern edge of humanity's clumped network of platforms. "Either that, or was pushed." Porbal grimaced, and Mossa nodded. "Quite. Of the two possibilities . . . Well. I wanted to learn if there was any particular reason why someone might choose that platform to, err, say farewell from, as it were."

Porbal tutted. "Stepped off, how very sad. And horrible. I suppose he had some reason, though, even if they were reasons only in his own mind."

I noted the gender assumption, as I had noted Mossa's sudden emphasis on suicide, but I had from the beginning of this strange meeting decided to keep my hands in my lap and my eyes on my hands, when not firmly fixed on the map.

"As for that platform . . ." The geographer (I saw through my lowered lashes) made a show of peering at the map. "Obviously it's the easternmost on that line, but you could hardly have missed that. There are still people who hold beliefs about the edges of the known world, in one direction or another. Isolated, of course; more so than the stations on other lines that might be further east."

"It may be no more than that," Mossa said agreeably, and made as if to stand.

"But also," Porbal put in, too smug to be hasty in trying to keep her attention, "we could consider the currents." He pulled a device from an internal pocket and tapped and grumbled and clicked at it for a few moments. "Hmm, yes. Now, we know well that someone who steps off a platform is likely to arrive, sooner rather than later, at a depth of the planet that will see their mortal remains utterly crushed and compacted. Naturally they would have already frozen to death at that point," he added. "But it's true that the strong winds and encircling forces, particularly out of the way of our rails, would carry someone in various directions, and it's easy for an amateur to calculate, for example, that stepping off at that particular point might lead their remains to be swallowed up in the Mighty Tempest." He shrugged, dismissive. "It wouldn't happen, of course; nor can I see that it would matter. But if someone is at the point of being ready to step off a platform, well, they may find significance in such things."

"Indeed," Mossa said thoughtfully. "That may perhaps be the key to it. Thank you very much. And might I trouble you to send me those calculations?"

"But of course," he said, rising in her wake. We bid him farewell at the door and returned to my rooms.

"And now our tea will be stewed and there is barely time for you to rest before dinner. But I hope that answered some of your questions." I said it with a sidelong look; I was fairly sure the answers she sought from Professor Porbal were not directly the ones she asked for.

Mossa flashed me a grin. "Indeed! But we can discuss that later. For now, the sensory experience at Slow Burn will be plenty of rest and refreshment for me. We had better go."

I was already tugging gently at her shirt; once satisfied that the injuries did not look any worse, and after a sadly hurried tea, I let her persuade me out into the night.

Chapter 9

Slow Burn was, most exceptionally, in the center of a small but dense wood. The owner had purchased soil, and saplings, and cultivated the fastest-growing firewood species she could find, all within her small allotted plot on Valdegeld platform. Tiny paths led through the trees to a slender building, and within the visitor found a long hearth, finished and partially enclosed in different configurations along its length for optimum efficiency in various approaches to cooking over woodfire. The tables followed the hearth, keeping the building long and narrow and also warm, and the menu changed constantly, although it usually included at least some of the carefully seeded byproducts of the tiny forest: morels, or mosses, or wild ginger. There was also wine, although that did not, sadly, come from local grapes, those still being beyond the range of possibility; Mossa had opted instead for the cedar-infused fermented sorrel liquor, and I joined her.

It was not until after the rich, herbed soup that either

of us made a move to speak, but once warmed and fed I found my mind replaying the strange interview we had just undergone, and, "I take it you still want to talk to a Modern geographer tomorrow? A second opinion, perhaps?"

Mossa laughed, sharp and surprised. "You noticed, eh?" She shook her head, still chuckling. "*Very* eager to talk to us, that Professor."

"I suppose—" I began, intending to ask her whether she was inclined to believe Bolien's disappearance to be suicide, but her eyes darted down the long room and I lowered my voice and adjusted my question. "Was your work today successful?"

Her eyes gleamed at me over the rim of her glass. "Suggestive, highly suggestive. Unfortunately," she lowered her voice as well, and with the crackle of the wood fire so near I was certain we should not be overheard, "I think it quite likely Rechaure's killer has already fled—"

"The significance of the rail station!" I exclaimed, though I remembered to do it quietly.

"Ye-e-es," Mossa said slowly. "Not the only significance of it. But yes, I believe the malefactor departed by railcar shortly after delivering the killing blow to the poor wretch. However, I have hopes we may yet triangulate on the evildoer."

"Well done, indeed," I said, raising my glass to her, although in truth I was a bit dismayed by the *we*. I had thought she would look in briefly on this case before returning to her other purpose, the one I could assist with; the plural pronoun suggested instead she would be continuing to assist the other Investigators.

We were silent as the plates were removed and replaced.

"Although," Mossa said, suddenly returning to my earlier

point, "I'm not sure we will go see the Modern geographers, not immediately."

"But I thought—"

"It's true that I preferred not to present my queries to— the scholar we saw today. But I am concerned that we may be lacking some information from the Preservation Institute. We may need to return there tomorrow."

"Ah," I said, somewhat puzzled. But it was probably a good idea to look into the feline attack; perhaps that was her intention. Or did she expect some new evidence about Bolien's activities there, before his fateful railcar journey and disappearance? In any case she did not seem inclined to speak further in the restaurant, which while it whetted my curiosity was probably wise, and so we sat in silence through most of that course.

"Tell me more about your studies," Mossa said. She spoke slowly, as if the alcohol was affecting her, or perhaps injuries and exhaustion. "I know what you do, of course, but . . ."

I looked at her in surprise; it was unlike Mossa to even hint at any gap in her knowledge, at least unless she was trying to draw someone out. "You have no idea what I do, do you?"

"You use Classical documents to analyze ancient Earth ecosystems, in the hopes . . ."

"In the hopes that we can get the balance of organisms right on one of our earlier tries," I finished. "Correct. My specific project—"

"Why . . . what does that mean, exactly?"

I stared again: did she not know? Or was this an attempt to show an interest in my work that she didn't feel?

Mossa gestured. "Yes, it's always being talked about,

this grand project of Classical scholarship. But why is it so important to get it right? Ecosystems adjust, don't they? I mean, obviously not always." That was impossible to deny. "But don't they tend towards balance? Why must it be so precise?"

"Mm," I said, thoughtfully. It was true that this fundamental was often taken as a given, and might be obscure to people outside the field. "Even an ecosystem that is not viable in the long-term, that *cannot* adjust itself sufficiently to find balance, may take some decades, or centuries, to die out, yes? And if we try to tweak it towards survival, that is far more complicated than starting from essentially nothing. And either way is still faster than seeding the tiniest single-celled microorganisms and waiting for millennia for everything else to develop. So the hope is that if we can mimic an ecosystem balance that existed on Earth before, that was relatively sustainable as long as people weren't horrible"—we both grimaced and then drank at that caveat—"then we can get back there ourselves much sooner."

"Yes, that is clear," Mossa agreed. "And you were saying about your specific project?"

"Ah yes. I study the British Isles, in the mid-twentieth century. At the moment I'm working on a *very* useful book about rabbits and their adventures. There's a wealth of descriptions of the flora and fauna in a highly circumscribed, clearly identified area. Truly amazing stuff, most astoundingly useful for us. And most incredibly, this book—a story book, note, perhaps even intended for children—has pages and pages of writing mentioning, oh, different flowers, and tiny beasts, and the author assumes that every organism he mentions is familiar to the readers. He barely describes any of it, because everyone he can imagine reading it already knows."

Mossa gave a little shudder, and I grinned at her. "So we mine the book for all the data we can squeeze out of it about where different species lived and how many and their relationships—have you any idea of the range of plants wild rabbits might eat?—and then we cross-reference with other books of roughly the same time and place and do it again, and again, and in this way build up an idea . . ."

"Of how to recreate an entire ecosystem, or a thousand, all at once instead of waiting out the many missteps of evolution."

"Naturally," I went on, for this subject always brought out my enthusiasm, "we will be combining our findings with those of the theoretical biologists, for example, and the forensic geologists, and so on."

"Admirable," Mossa murmured, and through the warmth brought on by her regard I looked her over with some concern. She was nearly slurring her words and I thought she must be more exhausted than I had imagined.

"Perhaps we had better skip dessert," I suggested, though in truth I had high hopes of the promised tart.

"Nonsense," Mossa responded, rousing herself. "Simply because I express some praise for your worthy endeavors does not mean I am hallucinating, Pleiti." I let the doubt show in my face, more to tease her than anything else, and after a few bites she rejoined, "Was I *so* self-centered during university?"

"You are what you are," I said; although in university, I must admit, that had not been my attitude. "Your intensity—your single-minded attention—yes, at times, it can be, er, it can obscure some of the niceties. But when one is the focus of that intensity—"

I stopped suddenly, aware that I was heated, and hoping the ruddy play of the firelight over my face would hide the heightened rush of the blood through my veins.

"It has lately occurred to me," Mossa began after a pause, "that perhaps I should be more intentional in how I direct my attention."

Our plates were removed again, which allowed me time to absorb the idea that Mossa, too, was considering her interactions in a different way than when we were students. It was with some relief that I saw the new dishes contained the awaited tart, and that we were on the last course.

"Work is . . . easier," Mossa went on. "That is, parts of it. The reports, the, the, *consideration* in the midst of a case . . ."

"Because it doesn't involve dealing with people," I agreed, taking a forkful.

She stared at me. "You understand?"

I laughed, I couldn't help it. "Mossa. My workdays are spent reading books written by the long dead about a healthy planet flowering with plants and animals. Yes, it is escapist, and antisocial as well."

She sputtered a laugh but stopped suddenly, eyeing me as though I had given her an idea. "What?" I asked, but she shook her head, hurrying her next forkful, and responded only, "Let's get back."

I insisted she bathe again but did not presume to go into the room; either she was able to reach the punctures herself to wash them or she did not think it was necessary, for she did not call me. She did allow me to check the wounds after she emerged, damp and warm, in my spare dressing gown. She slid the sleeves off her shoulders so that I could look: the dark points where the claws had sunk in were clean and even, with no discoloration or swelling, and I had no excuse to touch.

"They will make lovely scars," I said, for lack of anything better, and immediately berated myself for a statement so simultaneously banal—the worst sin, for Mossa—and over-personal—probably the second worst.

To my surprise, she didn't seem annoyed. "You think so?" She stretched and twisted her back as if to look at them, her muscles supple and rippling under her skin.

"Oh yes," I managed, making foolish gestures in the air as though to paint them. "The not-quite symmetry, the animal resonance with our epigenetic fears . . . that is, there's a mirror in my room if you would like to look."

I had not placed the mirror in my room (for the thought struck me, as I followed her in, that it could be seen as vain); the rooms had come furnished and it had never occurred to me to move it. Mossa didn't seem to mind, although she found it difficult to get a full view of her back in any case.

In another person I would have thought it flirting, but if Mossa had wanted me again she would have said so, or acted on it, reaching out to me as she turned from the mirror and asking license only just before her mouth met mine . . .

Instead she shrugged after a mere moment of over-the-shoulder efforts with the mirror, and walked past me towards the door.

I thought she was gone, and had released half of the

enormous breath I was holding when she spoke from the doorway. "Pleiti, I . . . I hope I'm not disturbing your work too much, by being here."

"Of course not," I said without thought, but she went on. "If you can spare the time, I do appreciate your help in this matter. It is even—it is invaluable, I should say."

I stared at her for a moment. "It's my pleasure, of course," I said, inanely, and her brows twitched. "All right, I enjoy it," I said, leaving off the politeness. "It's a change from my normal days, and quite frankly fascinating. Truly."

She nodded, and was gone. It took me longer to drag my gaze away from the door where she had stood, and all the while that I disrobed, and for most of the night while I lay in bed, I wondered whether I was wrong. Surely she would not use me, play with my affections so that I would assist her? No, Mossa would know that she did not have to, and she could be thoughtless but she was not needlessly cruel. So was I wrong, then? Was she, perhaps, hesitating to say what she wanted?

Or was she only oblivious? That was far more in her character, as I understood it.

Chapter 10

In the morning, over the now customary scones and tea, we looked over the attributes of the Modern geographers who had offered their services should we pass by their offices. "I do think we need to return to the Preservation Institute first," Mossa said, "but we may need to talk to one of these scholars sooner rather than later, so we may as well put them in order so we know where to go."

"But before we leave for the mauzooleum," I said, taking advantage of her distraction with a scone, "can you tell me what you are looking to learn? Since yesterday's meeting was all misdirection." It might not be strictly appropriate for her to tell me all the details, since I wasn't an Investigator, but since I was assisting her surely she could give me some parameters.

"Perhaps it's best," Mossa said, swallowing her mouthful, "if I tell you what I discovered yesterday about Rechaure's murder."

I didn't quite see how that would be helpful, or even

ethical, since that wasn't the case I was assisting her with, but I didn't want her to change her mind about telling me *something,* so I kept quiet and poured more tea.

"They took me first to the station, to see where he was found. Miserable day that it was yesterday, it was drafty and cold within the station, glowing gusts of elemental fog blowing everywhere. The waiting room, as you well know, is only slightly more sheltered than the platform."

I nodded, with a grimace; I always avoided the waiting room if I possibly could, preferring to arrive only just before my chosen railcar left. For one thing, one was sure to see just the tutor—in our student days—or colleague one did *not* want to meet, and then be stuck there ages with them; for another, it was a dreary place.

"It is, however, hardly ever empty, although in the darkest hours of the night it may be sparse. It seemed indeed unlikely that anyone should have been killed there, as the Investigators had themselves concluded from the lack of blood. I posit that they—probably two people, although one strong person could have managed it—killed Rechaure elsewhere, and brought him in under guise of helping a drunk or sleeping friend. It was still risky though! Certainly to have brought him all the way from his normal corner would have been extremely so. Therefore Rechaure was probably not there. Where was he? I knew that Rechaure usually would repair to the hostel when weather threatened, so I went there to ask."

"Had he stayed there?" I had found myself, despite her dry and circuitous telling, hanging on the tale.

"In fact, they were closed last night!"

"So he could not have gone there! Was it an unexpected closing or would he have known?"

"An excellent question, Pleiti!" Mossa eyed me consideringly, and I felt my face heat. "Do you know, I think you're wasted on these questions of ancient ecosystems?" I tried to sputter something about the urgency of my work, and how her talents, in fact, would be better spent—but she was already continuing. "The hostel had been undergoing renovations for some days. They were hoping to be finished by two days ago, but they were not."

"So he might have known this was a possibility?"

"Indeed he did. If you remember the other incongruity, it was that he left his things—his blankets, his sign—at the corner. That seemed unlikely to me if he was expecting to be away all night and day. As it turned out, I was able to speak to one of the receptionists at the hostel, who had seen Rechaure and informed him that he couldn't stay there." Mossa paused. "She was quite disturbed to learn he had later been killed, sans abris."

"Naturally she was!"

"It isn't as if she could have known. And she was very helpful. Apparently after he learned the hostel was still closed he went away down Blinkstart, but not the way he had come, the other way, and she was fairly sure he turned on Weilo."

"As if he were heading for the station," I exclaimed.

"Precisely. Perhaps he thought the waiting room was his best option for spending the night, although in that case I think he would have gone back for his blankets. More likely he wished to confirm the schedule of railcars, or something of the sort."

"And then?" I felt a chill as I asked it. Of course the hostel worker had been upset to learn he had been killed. I had been upset to learn he had been killed. And yet, there had been a kind of distance to it, and in this careful unraveling of his last hours and the decisions leading to his death, that distance was diminishing.

Mossa tapped her fingers. "It seems to me that he met someone on the platform, or recognized someone, shall we say. And that was his undoing." She chewed the last bite of scone, took a quick swallow from her tea cup, and stood. "Come! We must get to the Preservation Institute before it gets too late."

As we passed it on our way to the rail station I glanced at Rechaure's old corner long enough to see that his possessions had been removed, then averted my eyes, feeling obscurely guilty. For not knowing as much about him as Mossa did? For looking with curiosity instead of compassion? For not feeling as much loss as I might have?

We once again had our own compartment. It might have felt repetitive, going back to the mauzooleum, but the atmosphere between us had changed. On our last visit I had been stiff, unsure; now, while I didn't know exactly how close she wanted me, the old comfort of our university days was back. I relaxed against the seat, looking out the window at the fog. With the storm past, I could see a faint glow easing around the layers of thinner clouds still above us; leaning my head against the window to peer upwards I could even make out the crescent edge of Europa glimmering in the darkness.

At the administrative building Mossa asked for a meeting with Cyla, but when we were ushered into the selected room Cyla was accompanied by a sparse-bearded man, and I felt Mossa come even more alert beside me. He introduced himself as Frefor, Director of Operations, and he had hardly finished speaking when Mossa spoke.

"What has gone missing?"

Frefor and Cyla looked at each other, and Mossa's frustration grew. "Something has disappeared, that you have become aware of since last we spoke. Or is there some other reason that we now merit higher-level attention?"

Frefor was one of those men who must always make noises before they speak, like a short runway allowing their thoughts to launch. "We wanted to apologize to you for the situation with the caracal, and update you on its . . ."

Mossa made a dismissive gesture. "You recovered the animal? You have not discovered who was responsible? Very well, we can speak of that later, and if you have any evidence I would be happy to examine it, but the question of what else you have lost is far more urgent."

Frefor looked at Cyla (who appeared much calmer) with a moue of disgust; ignoring him, she answered: "It's true, I'm afraid. Several specimens are missing."

"Not live animals?" Mossa replied, over my gasp (I had expected . . . I don't know what, but a theft from the mauzooleum was shocking).

Frefor cleared his throat and thus inserted himself again. "We have already spoken to the Investigators Bureau in Sumberlan, they promised, they absolutely promised us that they would keep the secret . . ."

"And no less will I," Mossa replied impatiently. "Surely it would be better that I, already somewhat involved—"

"I wouldn't go so far as involved," he objected, but she continued without pause.

"—and on site, with additional information—"

"I'm sure at this point," Cyla broke in, with a warning

look at Frefor, still burbling like a coffeepot, "we would be very happy of your help."

Mossa acknowledged this only with a nod. "Not live animals?"

Frefor warmed up his voice box and responded. "No, no. Er, perhaps. I can't swear to every ant we have on site." It was, possibly, an attempt at humor, which Mossa ignored effortlessly. "No, a number of frozen germinate cells have disappeared from where they were kept . . ."

"Were they singular copies?" I burst in, over whatever Mossa was trying to say.

"No, no," Frefor replied, soothingly. "There are multiple extant copies of everything. We have at least two of everything here, one copy in the central vault and one"—he glanced at Cyla, then Mossa, then back to me, impressing us all with his consideration in revealing this—"attached to the habitat of each animal, or in the relevant center— insect, oceanic, and so on—if it's an animal we haven't reanimated." He made his coughy throat-clearing noise again and explained: "We learned from previous conservation efforts the folly of keeping everything in a single central bank that may suffer catastrophic failures of various kinds. In addition, there are copies at Stortellen—and a number of genetic maps, if not full copies, at Valdegeld as well," he added, with a nod at me.

"Where were the missing instances in this case stolen from?" Mossa asked, and clarified, "From the central vault here or from the habitats?"

"Oh, the habitats," Frefor replied, and frowned. "Which perhaps explains the odd configuration of what was taken: they must have grabbed what they could find. Although some of it was quite scattered throughout our constellation of platforms."

After some wrangling, Mossa was able to extract from him the promise of both the list of stolen cells and a map notating which had come from where; or, more accurately, Cyla was able to catch Mossa's eye and indicate that she would provide them as soon as Mossa stopped antagonizing Frefor and she could get him out of the way.

"Sorry about him," Cyla whispered, as she passed the map to Mossa and the list to her device. "He's very protective of the Institute, and—and, well, it's true. This theft could be devastating."

"But they're not unique," I said. "Surely you can reproduce the specimens . . ."

"Oh yes," Cyla agreed. "But there are many people who would love to see us discredited for lack of security precautions, and it might be enough to end our protections and lead to the repurposing of our platform space."

"Have you considered," Mossa asked dryly as she folded away the map into her pocket, "that it may be one of those people who is behind the theft?"

"Oh, surely not," Cyla replied, and then reconsidered. "That is, it seems so indirect. I'm sure that there are people who would pay for such samples, even if they're not unique; that would be a much more immediate reason for the theft. And the people who would benefit if we lost our status . . . well, they're all . . ."

"Not the people you imagine to be common thieves?"

Cyla smiled wryly. "Uncommon thieves, perhaps." She sighed. "You're right, it's possible, and we'll need to consider it, but that does complicate things."

"And you haven't received any response in regards to Bolien's activities here before he disappeared?"

"No, sorry, I meant to mention that to you, but no, nobody responded to say they had met with him." Her eyes widened. "But—surely you don't think—"

"Is it possible that he stole the samples? Or did they disappear after he left?"

Cyla shook her head, her expression suggesting she had quite a lot to consider after this conversation. "They could have been taken any time in the last week."

Mossa nodded, then asked to see where the caracal had been released, although she clearly had low expectations about what was to be found there.

Chapter 11

"How could he be so dismissive?" I expostulated, when we were finally alone.

We were on a remote platform, large enough for a medium-sized cat to run and pounce within its confines, and connected to the rest of the mauzooleum by stairs going up and down. It was far from the visitor's path though; I wondered how the cat had found us, or been aimed at us.

Mossa was examining the container, built into one of the long bars surrounding the habitat, that held the caracal's genetic identicals, proto-caracals in cell form. They hadn't been stolen, but I assumed she wanted to get an idea of what the containers were like. "Who? Oh that . . . director, or whatever he was? It happens." She was commendably dismissive herself. "There are plenty of people who don't like Investigators, and particularly don't like to see someone like myself leading their investigations."

"Oh surely—" I began, and Mossa looked up with a face etched into blankness.

"Forgive me, Pleiti, but I believe your experience in Valdegeld may not be typical of the entire planet." That silenced me, and before I could recover to argue the premise—I *had*, after all, spent years away from the closed environ of the university before achieving my position, and the Preservation Institute *should* reflect academic attitudes, and so was my milieu as much as hers—Mossa had moved on to the place where the caracal had emerged from its habitat. The mostly transparent barrier had been re-closed with a temporary fastening. "Hm. Of course they've made too much of a mess fixing this for me to see much here. But perhaps . . ."

She turned to examine the bit of platform we stood on, and started walking in the direction which, I knew from my map, was the most direct route to where we were attacked. Again and again she knelt to the surface of the platform, and frowned. Finally, just up a small flight of stairs from where we had been strolling—had it been only two days before?—she grunted with a sort of triumph. "Here."

I squatted reluctantly beside her, feeling my knees creak. "See these scratches?" Mossa reached into her bag and pulled out a crumple of cloth. A crumple of *blood-stained* cloth, I realized, recoiling.

"Mossa! Is that—"

She was already straightening out the shirt, aligning the punctures in the cloth with the damage to the metal of the platform. "Yes. The last claw did not find much purchase, but these are clearly from the same—"

"A caracal's claws are retractable," I pointed out, having

looked this information up during the long period of wakefulness after cleaning her wounds that night. "Why would it leave claw marks on the ground?"

Mossa looked up at me, her eyes bright and present above her atmoscarf. "Why indeed? In fact, that hint of a mark here is more telling than the lack of scratches up till this point. It seems that something made the feline angry just before it touched the ground here."

I considered that. "Someone carried it here, harassed it somehow, and—"

"Pointed it at us." Mossa wrinkled her nose. "I concur. Still not a very efficient or certain method of assassination, or even injury."

"If they were stealing the cells, and happened to notice us and launch the attack on impulse . . ." I stopped, remembering that the timing didn't work out.

"Possible," Mossa said, "but as you have clearly remembered, that would mean that it wasn't Bolien who stole the genetic material."

"It might not have been him," I argued weakly.

"It might indeed not have been. But then, why was he here at all?" Mossa shook her head. "There may be reasons for that we don't know, but while keeping an open mind, what looks most sensible to me now is that Bolien stole—or perhaps more accurately, received—the genetic material on his way east, where he disappeared. Our arrival here threatened whoever was working with him within the Institute, and they impetuously released the caracal."

She rose and started for the station, then stopped short, crouching again. "Or perhaps not so impetuously." She pulled a vacuum container from her coat and pressed it to the ground. When she held it up again shreds of organic material were visible inside. "That looks very much like catnip."

I was mostly silent on the return trip, and grateful for Mossa's reliable taciturnity. Bad enough that the Preservation Institute had lost materials; worse that it was in danger of closing; worst of all that someone within that august entity was implicated. (Could it have been the unpleasant Frefor? I wondered. But surely then he would have been both subtler and more effective). Or, no: for the more I thought the harder I found it to muster surprise over the fact that a person had proved corruptible. The worst was that the Institute for Earth Species Preservation might be lost. True, the very concept of the mauzooleum was extravagant, and unlikely, and extraneous; but there were few enough such spots on our planet, and it would be a sadder place without the glimpse of biodiversity offered at the Preservation Institute.

"And yet," Mossa said, across the compartment from me, "one has to wonder how the animals feel about it."

I gaped at her, first in incomprehension, then in disbelief. "How did you know what I was thinking?"

Her smile was almost sad.

"Your face, dearest Pleiti"—and my traitor face heated, though her expression warned me well enough that this was not a compliment, that the superlative was merely a drip of casual affection—"tells all, transparent as, oh, this window." She tapped it with her knuckles. "Particularly when you are upset, and when you are thinking through the logic of it."

I scrabbled away from the subject, too obviously. "So you have a theoretical narrative of the case, a plausible one." The thought that the investigation might soon be over weighed on me; I tried to modulate my voice into polite curiosity. "What are you going to do now?"

"Ah, but you forget: the theft at the Preservation Institute is not the case I am investigating."

"I had forgotten!" I admitted, cheered nonetheless as the puzzle gripped me again. "So, Bolien receives the stolen cells and then—what? Is overcome with guilt and steps off a platform, cells in hand? Or is pushed by—who? A rival? Certainly not by someone from the Preservation Institute, not without retrieving the material first? Or he was cornered?"

"All possibilities," Mossa responded, "but—as you admit by framing them into a question—all fairly unlikely. Consider another factor (that you have also forgotten, but then, it has been a busy few days): the lying geographer."

I considered this silently for some time. "He was involved, or else why would he lie?" I said at last. "But—"

"There was a conspiracy, one that reached beyond a simple bilateral deal between someone on the inside and someone without."

"Yes, that seems undeniable," I murmured. "You think the purpose was undermining the Preservation Institute as much as stealing the cells themselves? Certainly the particular materials that were stolen are not the ones that seem likely to garner the highest payoff."

Mossa brooded. "I think we will speak to another Modern Geographer after all. On our arrival, if possible."

Chapter 12

Once we had disembarked I led Mossa decisively towards the Modern faculty campus rather than back to my rooms. It was late afternoon, and the storm had left puddles in the shallow depressions of the weathered platform where pigeons were now splashing their iridescent feathers, but the weather had settled some. Weak sunlight filtered through the layers of natural and artificial atmosphere, warming me and making easier the determination to trek so far from the delights of the hearth.

When the first humans settled Giant, the atmoshields of the meager few initial platforms blocked out all weather, serving as hard shells that preserved oxygen and warmth and humidity at equally standard degrees. But while people *can* live like that—as proved by the spaceship- and space station–bound years before the platforms were ready in sufficient numbers—most don't like to, and when the porous atmoshield was developed it quickly became popular and soon standard on most platforms, despite the inconveniences of wind, rain, tempests, and variable temperatures.

My parents' platform, a remote midsized agricultural settlement, was fully atmoshielded, as many farming areas were (although lately I had noticed in the more expensive provisionaries in Valdegeld a trend to labeling some produce as "lightly atmoshielded," as though that conferred some particular benefit). Perhaps because of growing up in that environment I remained keenly aware and appreciative of the modulations of weather.

I doubt Mossa noticed the sunshine; she seemed entirely concentrated on her thoughts. I might have believed her interiority meant she was secreting detailed observations of our route and our surroundings, but when I caught a spark in the darkening sky she was oblivious to it until I jostled her with my elbow. "Look!" Another point of light spun by to the horizon. "They're setting a new ring?"

Mossa glanced up, waiting to see the next segment flash past. "Ah yes. I had heard one was imminent. Around 6° I think, but the main crossing—with the 1°02'—is quite far west of Qirao."

"Opening up a lot of unconnected area, then." The human inhabitants—settlers, exiles, or refugees as we variously thought of ourselves—on Giant had achieved quite a reasonable population over the past few centuries, but the surface—so to speak—area of Giant was so vast that while the carefully calibrated ring-rails necessarily circumnavigated the planet, platforms were clustered over less than a sixteenth of the sphere, and transportation time meant that adding a ring to the network was generally considered preferable to expanding platforms out along the existing rails.

The bright shuttles with their hidden arcs slid past, more frequent but slower as they approached the surface and their geosynchronous orbit. I thought about shooting stars and their descriptions in ancient Earth literature, thought of descriptions of railroads and explorers and barely habitable tracts of unsettled land.

"We always want more farmland, and more places to live," Mossa answered, as though it were self-evident and unexceptional, but she stood there with me anyway, watching until the flashes disappeared into the glow of the horizon.

I had an odd feeling, as we stood there next to each other, that we were watching *together*, almost as if we were holding hands. But I did not dare to stretch my fingers towards hers before she lowered her gaze to the road in front of her and set out again. She was so determined on her thoughts that I had to touch her shoulder to draw her attention to the entranceway of the building; my fingertips fizzed at the touch as though she were the frozen planetside face of a platform.

"In here," I said unnecessarily, to cover my awkwardness, my annoyance with myself, my superfluity.

Mossa stopped and faced me instead of continuing her charge straight in. "Pleiti," she said, and my whole self cringed in anticipation of the gentle let-down. I don't think I let it show in my face, but I wasn't meeting her eyes, either, and her voice when she continued was softer. "How would I do this without you?"

By the time I looked up she had turned and vanished into the building. I hesitated for a moment, because being of utility was more than I had expected, and yet one still does not want to be used. Of use, but not used. Before I could spiral into the philology of that observation, I followed her inside.

Mossa's questions to this Modern geographer did not include the missing man or his mindset. Instead, she asked her for the most up-to-date globe she had showing rail-rings and platforms, and pointed out the site from which Bolien had disappeared, serviced by a single line.

"Can you show me where this line intersects any line leaving from Valdegeld's main station?"

The Modern Geographer was a tall broad woman with a wide-angle face and a ready smile, now slightly dimmed as she wondered why this Investigator was asking her something she could have calculated from any rail guide, with a bit of time and effort. Nonetheless, she gave Mossa the list, and followed it uncomplainingly with a list of secondary intersections, points that could be gained from both termini with only one change. Mossa examined the lists deliberately; whether she found any meaning in them I did not learn until later. She looked up and asked another question, pointing again at the platform where Bolien had vanished. "How long would it take to get to the next platform from here if you went east?"

We both stared at her, the geographer in befuddlement, myself in the astonishment of sudden understanding.

"East? There are no railcars going further east than that platform. They stop there and return west. There are no platforms further east."

"But if you wanted to, if you hired a private railcar, for example, and took it east until you reached . . ." Mossa spun the globe, a gesture I suspected of being pure drama since she must have already memorized the name she needed, and pointed at what is normally considered the westernmost platform on the 4°63' ring. "Sapilvest, how long would that take?"

The geographer eyed the long arcing gap between platforms doubtfully. "It would be very stormy, you know. Uncomfortable, to say the least. But I suppose it would take . . . let's see, there would be no stops either . . . about twelve to sixteen days, I should say, depending on the type of railcar."

"*Local* days?"

"Of course," she said, proud of it, while I tried not to roll my eyes: Modernists were so fiercely Giant-oriented in all their terminology.

Mossa thanked her, asked her not to mention our visit if it could be avoided, and we took our leave.

Night had fallen while we spoke to the geographer. "Shall we find something to eat?" I asked as the door closed behind us.

Mossa frowned. "There isn't time."

"Oh come now, Mossa, you have to eat." I cast about for a close restaurant. "There's a tubular place nearby—or if you would rather go back to the rooms and work there, we can always order."

With a grudging glance at the moons wheeling in the sky she agreed to the former, and we soon had our cylindrical layers of protein and flavorings in hand. "Where to now?" I asked, and realized as I did that Mossa either hadn't decided yet or didn't think I would like it, since otherwise she would already be leading the way.

"Pleiti," she said, and said it the same way she had at

the entrance to the Modern Geographer's. I steeled myself again. "Pleiti, you have been so helpful to me, I was wondering if you would mind researching something."

"But of course, Mossa," I said, still a bit wary. "Research is what I do."

She nodded. "Well then, I think we should split up. If you could look into the people who might benefit from the closing of the Preservation Institute, and make a list of them."

"And cross-reference, perhaps, with any contacts of Professor Porbal?"

"Porbal!" It burst out from her with something like a laugh. "Yes, I'd forgotten about him, but you're quite right. He might be the unwitting key."

"Very well, Mossa," I said. "I don't know why you're so chary about asking me, it's quite reasonable. What will you be doing?"

"Following up another thread."

"Enigmatic," I observed genially to a large grasshopper that was perched on a wrought fence along the street we were pacing.

"I am not sure it's correct," Mossa replied. "But I'll tell you if it comes off."

"All right then," I said. "Meet back at my rooms in a few hours?"

With a nod, we were each on our way.

Chapter 13

I turned my steps generally towards the university center while I thought about the best place and method for pursuing my quarry. Of the first there was really no great question. Valdegeld had a number of excellent libraries, but while each might receive such broadsheets and other current documents as were in general circulation, only one, the library under Faistel Heights, had any real specialization in Modern concerns. It was not far, as I was already on the Modern side of campus, and I hastened my steps until I saw the looming bulk of Faistel, its sides crenellated with the fashion, more than a century old now, of using incompletely smashed motor vehicles from Earth as building material.

There were times in Earth's history when "modern" suggested something that might be less comfortable, perhaps of lesser quality. While it was true that Modern areas of study—those focusing on our current planetary

home, rather than the pre-exile history back on Earth—
were far less prestigious than the Classical, that distinction did not extend fully to the facilities. Faistel Modern
Library was quite as well appointed as Uiven, the refer-
ence area I usually used. There were warming chairs and
semi-autonomous carrels and borrowable blankets and
a central art exhibit, as well as the makings of quite decent tea.

It was, therefore, not an unpleasant evening, except
for my growing awareness of how many people would be
happy to rid our planet of the mauzooleum and the more
insidious suspicion, rapidly becoming all but certainty,
that Mossa was up to something.

I stopped my perusal of recently approved platform
exploitation permits to consider why I thought that, and
mentally produced the following list:

1. *She stopped twice, once on the way into the Geographer's and once on the way out, as if indecisive
   or reconsidering; ergo, she was doing something she
   didn't want to do or felt guilty about.*
   *a) This occurring both before and after we spoke to
   the geographer meant our discussion there did not
   change her reluctance, but perhaps confirmed it?*
2. *Come to think of it, she had been generally distracted even before we got to the geographer's.*
3. *She hadn't wanted to eat, a sign that she was in
   pursuit of something—physical or conceptual.*
   *a) And yet, she had let me convince her. That was
   odd. It constituted, perhaps, a new willingness to
   admit to her own physical needs?*

I considered this list. Hardly conclusive. Perhaps the geographer's information hadn't mattered at all? And yet, she had stopped in just the same way after we exited.

I found a globe of the Modern world—handy, as it turned out, to be in the Modern Library—and followed the ring Mossa had indicated away from civilization and settlements. As our population grows there is always talk of expanding further around the curves of the rings we have, rather than adding more rings to make this area denser and more interconnected, but most people want to be close to existing facilities or require such proximity for their enterprises. My parents, for example, were hardly social ants, and enjoyed their relative isolation, but they still needed to acquire inputs and transport their crops to where they were needed; settling farther away would increase travel delays. As today's Modern geographer had noted, the time it takes to circumnavigate Giant is simply too daunting.

But that is exactly what Mossa's questions suggested had been done. Bolien had disappeared by doing something so entirely unexpected that no one even thought of it. I counted the local days since his disappearance: yes, he should be returning to civilization about now, assuming his railcar (another problem: how had the people on that isolated platform not noticed the railcar?) hadn't failed somehow, and why should it? And if he was back, where would he go?

It was easy enough to recreate the list the Geographer had given Mossa by looking for the intersections and secondary intersections of that ring with the line from our main station (but why did she think it should intersect with the line from Valdegeld Main Station? Why not one of our other stations? Why Valdegeld at all?), but none of the

platform names on the list leapt out at me as significant.
Then again, several of them I had never heard of or knew
next to nothing about.

I was tapping my chin with my stylus, wondering if it was
worth reading up on each of the possible platforms, when
another thought came to me as clearly as if someone was
speaking in my ear: *had Mossa responded in any way to confirm my suggestion of meeting back in my rooms?*

She had said nothing.

Had she nodded when I did?

I replayed the moment in my head, the glow of the gaslights in the dimness, the sky just dark enough overhead
for Io's eruptions to sparkle in the dusk, Mossa's restrained
gaze meeting mine.

She hadn't.

Suddenly furious, I shoved my research results into
my satchel. On impulse, I added the globe, and then a rail
timetable as well. I hesitated over this last for a moment,
wondering if I should check the scheduled routes before
I committed myself to action, but I wasn't positive which
platform I would be traveling to and a delay at this moment could be decisive. Sprinting in an undignified man-
ner from the library, I emerged to the darkened streets and
ran for the station.

It was close to midnight, and the railcars were somewhat
fewer than at dusk or dawn, but there were still enough
departures to fill up the board, and enough people in the
cavernous station that I had to thread through them, peering
in all directions, looking for Mossa. I knew I might be

wrong; or she might be already on a railcar. She might, I thought with my stomach dropping, already have left. I glanced at the board again: the next departure was on the 0°25' line, in three minutes. I didn't think that was one of the rings that intersected with the one from which Bolien had disappeared—I was almost sure—but at this time of night perhaps it offered connections that would arrive at the right platform faster than something more direct—I tugged the timetable partly out of my satchel, then dropped it back in and ran for the andén instead.

I climbed on the railcar and swung along the corridor, glancing into every compartment. When the whistle blew I was only halfway down the cars, but I got off anyway, and stood despondent on the andén as the railcar swept into motion, smooth and poised on its ring. Mossa had probably left already—or maybe I was inventing things, and I would find her innocently waiting for me back in my rooms. I snorted at that image, and made my way towards the andén of the next departing railcar. I was still panting and hot from my run, so I walked slowly, my atmoscarf wrapped tightly to keep the moisture softening my air.

I tried to be logical about it. I should check the waiting room—would Mossa wait in a place she knew to be the scene of a recent murder? Yes, of course she would—but first I needed to triage the rest of the railcars on the departure board. I scanned it carefully, and yes: the next one to leave was traveling west on the 3°42', which I was fairly confident intersected the 4°63' west of here, although I couldn't remember the name of the platform. I began to hurry again, feeling slightly hopeful. The departure wasn't for another twenty-two minutes; indeed I saw, when I got to the andén, the railcar hadn't arrived yet.

And there was Mossa, waiting for it.

I slowed so that I could approach her without gasping for breath. She was facing away from me, her atmoscarf pulled up high under her short scruff of hair, and—my anger flared again—she was carrying her valise. I wanted to approach her calmly, as calmly as she had responded to me when I told her I was ending our love affair back in university, but I am not Mossa.

"No farewells?" I screeched.

She turned, and I thought there was a brief softening of her expression, as if she almost smiled. "Pleiti!" My name in her mouth no longer sounded like the prelude to some harsh truth; it sounded, rather, as if she were pleased to see me. Though, perhaps, not particularly surprised. "You made it!"

My jaw ached. "Made it? You didn't tell me you were leaving!"

Mossa glanced around us, though I was sure she already knew the precise number of people on the andén (I cannot myself be more specific than *few if any*). "To be—to be truthful"—I knew as she said this that she too was reliving that last fight at university, when I had accused her of frequently being dishonest without lying—"I was hoping you would come, but I wasn't sure I should. Hope for it, that is, or tell you, or invite you."

"Why," I gritted out, "not?"

"Well, it's sure to be dangerous," Mossa said, somewhat abashedly. "And, beyond that, it's my job, you know. You have your own work, very important work, which I've been taking you away from for the past few days." A movement in the dimness caught my eye: the railcar, approaching in the distance, illumination glowing from its windows. Even in the midst of that anguished conversation, the warmth and shelter promised by those remote and moving lights tugged at me.

"We talked about this," I said, with difficulty. "Choices. Each person gets to make their own choices. I don't care how smart you are, *I'm not stupid*."

"Of course you aren't," Mossa said, as if indignant that I should suggest it. "You figured out where to find me."

It wasn't the sideways praise that disarmed me so much as her lack of guilt or responsive anger. I let my arms and shoulders drop, my eyes on the railcar as it advanced, slowing. "What is this danger you mentioned? You do realize, by the way, that if you had *told* me what to plan for I might have had time to go home and get a change of clothes."

"Not to worry." Mossa thumped the side of her valise as the railcar slid to a stop beside us. "I brought some of your things, just in case."

"You packed *my* clothes for a trip you didn't bother to tell me about?"

"I really did hope you would come." Why could she melt me so easily? "Shall we?" Mossa tilted her head towards the open door of the railcar emanating light and warmth.

I followed her in.

Chapter 14

The deliciously thawing warmth, the cushioning of the soft seat against my back, the hypnotic swirling of gasses against the window pane—all these lulled me, and it was some time before I stirred myself to ask Mossa, who appeared similarly at ease across from me, the most basic of questions: "Where are we going?"

Mossa blinked slowly as though emerging from a long chain of thought. "It's a platform called Frontel—oh, well done," she interjected, as I reached into my bag and pulled out the globe and then the timetable. "Perhaps you can add to my unfortunately scant knowledge about the place."

"How did you identify it?" I flipped through the section of the timetable offering brief descriptions of all the platforms listed.

"As you heard—as you must have understood, to find me— I was looking for a platform on an intersection or, since those are few, on a second- or third-order intersection—

between Valdegeld Main Station and the ring from which Bolien disappeared. Once—"

"Yes, that," I interrupted. "Of course I understand why you are tracing the ring Bolien was last seen on, but why the main station?"

Mossa leaned back and tapped her fingers together. "Yes. Well. It is speculation at this point—which is the other reason I didn't tell you, this might be a useless trip—but I strongly suspect that Rechaure's murder and Bolien's disappearance are connected."

"But—how?" I sputtered, once I had recovered from my surprise.

"The suggestive fact," Mossa replied, her gaze trailing along the fog-strewn window, "is that Rechaure was killed at the station. There doesn't seem to be any particular reason for him to be killed, not at this point in time. So his unusual location is the most likely trigger. And *that* makes me think that he observed something indicating malfeasance, something related to Valdegeld. Now, I am willing to entertain the idea of multiple instances of malfeasance occurring at Valdegeld at any given time—" I snorted. "Quite. But enough to kill for? That seems unlikely. Ergo, it is not an unreasonable supposition that whatever Rechaure observed that led to him being killed was related to Bolien's disappearance. And if *that* is the case, then someone involved in the disappearance was departing from the main station."

"So Rechaure was just in the wrong place?" I asked, somehow saddened.

"There were other people around the station around that time as well, if not very many," Mossa answered. "It is possible he was the only one there during a very narrow critical moment, but it seems more likely that it was a combination of being in the wrong place and knowing the wrong person."

"Ah! That makes sense," I agreed. "Rechaure knew many of the people at the university by sight." The implication of that made my stomach sink. "You think someone else at the university is involved, besides Bolien."

"And Porbal," Mossa reminded me. "Yes, it seems likely, given the extensive links between the university and the Preservation Institute, as well as the low probability that Bolien interacted much with people *outside* of his social group. However, the university is too large, and travel too common, to easily trace who might have left from the main station that evening; also, if they killed Rechaure, they might have delayed their trip, although the decision to leave his body close at hand in the waiting room suggests not."

"And how did you narrow down the possibilities from there?"

Mossa leaned forward, pulling my attention back to her face, her proximity, but it was only to tap her finger on the timetable forgotten on my lap. I looked down and found the listing for Frontel:

A mid-sized gas compression factory, I read aloud, *now abandoned. Population: 0.*

I looked up at her face, still close to mine. "Suggestive, indeed."

My voice came out softer than I had planned.

"But only that," Mossa said, leaning back in her seat. "It may very well be that I am wrong, and this long journey is wasted." She gave me a brief smile. "Therefore I hesitated to invite you." Before I could respond to that she went on.

"What did you learn about those who might wish to close down the Preservation Institute?"

I brought out my list. "There are a number of people who have expressed formal interest in the past and have the resources to purchase at least some of the platforms—the Institute complex is enormous, it would almost certainly need to be sold as different lots. Or perhaps some core of it might remain." I had not at all come to terms with the idea of a Giant without the mauzooleum.

"Or perhaps purchased by a group or organization," Mossa agreed, studying the list. "Wasn't this group the one talking about establishing a new university?"

"Surely not in such proximity to Valdegeld!" I responded, more out of pique than realism. I ran down the rest of the list. "Then again, there's Selat Pintror." The innovator of a new platform design, ta had already invested in converting several existing spaces in hopes of persuading the organizing committees to contract with ta for new platforms. "Although I'd imagine there are easier acquisitions for someone like ta. Or maybe Iobila Het." Her water filtration systems had certainly put her in a position to buy large swaths of the Preservation Institute's territory, if she had a reason to do so. And perhaps pure obtainment was reason enough for some of these people.

"I did not have the time, unfortunately, to look into whether any of these people had any interaction with Bolien. To tell the truth," I admitted after a brief pause, "I'm not quite sure how I would go about doing so."

"Challenging," Mossa agreed, still eyeing the list. "Perhaps when we return we can look for professional associations and clubs and so on in common—assuming, that is, that the question is not resolved by then."

I could not repress a shiver. "You think we will find the malefactor at this"—I glanced at the description— "abandoned gas compression factory?"

"That is rather the idea."

"That seems astute, but at the same time unwise." She laughed outright at that; emboldened, I went on. "Really, Mossa, it does not seem the most propitious place to confront criminals—even if those criminals are well-educated thieves of inanimate cellular material intent on dastardly property piracy."

"If it's any comfort, my dear Pleiti"—my heart thudded— "I don't expect any of them still to be there. We will be searching only for clues, any possible hint—"

"Porbal!" I said suddenly.

". . . Yes?"

"We know—we strongly suspect he is part of the conspiracy. Could not he be the murderer of Rechaure?"

"Possible, of course," Mossa said, in a tone that meant *but highly unlikely.* "However, if we're assuming that the murderer did in fact leave for the rendezvous after doing away with Rechaure, it won't work, since the bad professor was still in Valdegeld to attempt to unrail us."

I subsided into my seat. "A numerous conspiracy, then."

"It is not impossible, I suppose," Mossa murmured, "that Porbal went and returned . . . although that would not give Bolien enough time to arrive, certainly . . . or perhaps I am wrong, and the rendezvous platform is closer . . ."

She was running through possibilities to herself, and I let my attention drift, first to the swirling gas outside the window, then to the platform descriptions on the page of the book open on my lap. I was idly imagining a visit to a place where *early experimental soils led to one of the most diverse insect populations on Giant, although the flora is unfortunately not quite as successful* when one of her sentences was clear enough again to catch my attention.

"I've often thought," Mossa mused, "that from an Investigator's perspective, it is a pity that there is no ticketing system for railcars."

It took me a moment to understand that. "What, pay? For railcar travel?"

"Don't sound so horrified," she said, amused. "You must be familiar with the concept from your Classical studies."

"Well, certainly," I said. "But firstly, we all know how that benighted civilization turned out, and secondly they lived on a planet where it was at least *possible* to walk from place to place."

Mossa's smile had broadened. "You're quite right, of course. Still, it would be nice to know who had traveled where, among our wide pool of suspects. You look done in, Pleiti," she said, her tone suddenly changing to concern. "You should rest. It's a long journey, and we don't know what awaits us at the end."

I was not energetic enough, at that point, to argue, except for the minor cavil of insisting that I check her back before we slept. The wounds were well scabbed by then and not inflamed, so I stretched myself on the bench, expecting her to do the same opposite. At the time I closed my eyes, however, she was still curled in the corner, staring out the window, her lips moving slightly as her marvelous brain ticked through the workings of the problem.

Chapter 15

When I woke, gas-shrouded daylight poured through the windows and the wall of the railcar was covered with a storyboard, although even as I opened my eyes Mossa was removing the laminate squares one by one.

"Figure anything out?" I asked, through a creaking yawn.

She glanced at me coolly but didn't bother to answer. "I was about to wake you. We'll be arriving in an hour, and you should prepare yourself."

"Oh yes," I said, propping myself into a sitting position and rubbing dried effluvia from my eyes. "You did mention some danger."

Mossa frowned. "I'm not certain. It seems unlikely that anyone would still be here . . . but we have only an estimate of Bolien's arrival. His contact may still be waiting, or we may come upon them both in the midst of their discussions. Although that seems unlikely; they should at least be aware of the railcar schedule and taking reasonable precautions when there is a stop."

Reasonable precautions might, it occurred to me, constitute the very danger she had worried about. "Is it not likely that one or both of them might board this railcar as it continues?" I asked.

"Very possible," Mossa said, looking pleased as she usually did when I came up with something that agreed with her thinking. "We must keep a close eye out at the station."

That established a fidgety quiet. I stared at the depleting cards of the storyboard. Noticing the one labeled, in large letters, *Mouzooleum* [sic—or an obscure joke of Mossa's?] reminded me of a thought I had entertained the night before, when I was too close to sleep to do anything about it.

"Is it possible," I offered, "that this conspiracy originates from the Preservation Institute, rather than the university?"

Mossa paused and turned to listen, although her expression did not suggest a lot of confidence in this theory. "And their actions lead to the Institute losing its territory?"

"Suppose someone working for the Preservation Institute *wanted* that to happen," I pushed on, "but they couldn't do it officially."

"Why would they want it to happen?"

I tried to think of a reason. "Perhaps they have come to the belief that the situation is cruel for the animals. Or maybe they benefit somehow, personally, if the Institute is closed . . ." That line of thought didn't lead me to any feasible theories. "Or they could be of the opinion that using all that space in the tenuous hope that seeing live animals will help us return to Earth is irresponsible, and it should be used to better the lives of people living on Giant now."

Mossa frowned at me. "Is this because you are still resentful of Frefor's demeanor?"

"Possibly," I admitted.

She waited a long moment, then somewhat grudgingly conceded, "It's not the most ridiculous narrative I've come up with. But I do wonder whether Rechaure would have so fatally recognized someone not from Valdegeld." She considered, then answered herself before I could. "Perhaps he might, if they visited often enough. Or perhaps he was killed for a different reason. I'll keep the theory in mind."

I subsided into my blankets, conjecturing about the more bizarre theories and attempting without success to fill in the gaps in what remained of the storyboard. I was still groggy from sleep, I realized, and thought I should recover from that before we arrived at the potential ambush.

"I'm going to the provisions car, if you want anything," I announced, wobbling to my feet.

"There's no provisions car, only an automat," Mossa informed me.

"Irradiated creakers," I replied, using Valdegeld student slang for infrequently traveled rings. "Well, I need tea anyway. Do you want some?"

Mossa did, and requested something sugary as well. I edged into the corridor and started walking towards the front of the railcar. We had had the corridor curtains closed in our compartment; the passage was brighter, and through the windows I could see pale writhing gasses, whipping by with enough force to tell me we were passing through a storm, though a minor one. The car swayed above its single rail, and I kept one hand out as I walked, prepared to grab the bannister along the wall.

Some of the compartments had closed doors, but none of the open ones held any sign of passengers, and by the time I reached the automat my nape was prickling. I selected the teas and a pallid pastry, glanced over my shoulder twice as the cups were filling, and juggled the lot back to the compartment.

"Unpopular line," I observed, handing Mossa her cup.

"Not much out here," she agreed after the first tentative sip. "You see why I didn't tell you."

I refused to do that. "So your idea was to vanish without leaving me any idea of where you had gone."

Again, shame skated over her face as though unfamiliar with the territory.

"The Investigators Bureau knows." She sipped and, perhaps because I said nothing, went on. "I can see how good Valdegeld is for you. But I don't think I could do it."

I thought furiously about how happy I was following her around to these different platforms, about how she seemed to enjoy the visit to Valdegeld, at least, well enough, but what came out was, in a snarl, "Nobody's asking you to."

Chapter 16

We were both poised and ready well before the railcar pulled in to the lonely station at Frontel. Mossa stepped off the carriage before it had fully stopped, peering up and down the andén while I hovered in the corridor of the railcar, listening for doors, footsteps, or any surreptitious movement. By the time I stepped down to the station we were both convinced no one had boarded or disembarked besides us. Looking around the empty, single-ring station I couldn't imagine why anyone would want to.

Mossa, however, was gesturing to me from the corner of the bereft station. I hurried towards her, observing the low flat ceiling, the simple wall, pierced with only one set of doors between the station and the rest of the platform. Old, cheaply built, and not lavished with care in the time since. We'd be lucky if it didn't crack off the ring and plunge into the depths of Giant while we were there.

I found Mossa was standing beside a narrow, curving

downwards ramp. "What's down there?" I asked, wrinkling my nose at the dimness of it.

Without answering—for of course, how should she know?—Mossa started down. With a sigh, I followed, wrapping my atmoscarf more tightly against the chill. To my relief, the passage opened up again only a short way down, and onto what looked like another andén, the mimic of the one—I glanced upwards—yes, that formed the ceiling above us. "What is this?"

Mossa strolled to the edge of the andén, peering up at the underside of the ring passing along it. Curious, I joined her, but the metal rail that circled the planet—that, with its fellows, kept us at a livable orbit of this inhospitable world—was the same burnished steel beneath as on the top. "Have you ever seen," Mossa began, "an old-fashioned railcar? There are a few examples in the museum on Yaste, I believe . . ."

She went on, but those words had been enough for my mind to conjure the picture of what she meant and, with it, make sense of the scene in front of us. "A *suspended* railcar?"

Mossa nodded. "Before the gyroscopic technology was perfected such vehicles were quite common, if not very comfortable."

I eyed her rather pleased, perhaps even smug mien. "You expected to find this?"

Mossa nodded. "I believe this explains how Bolien left the eastward platform without being seen."

I could feel my brows rising in disbelief. "You think he got on a suspended railcar? For a ride around the *planet*?"

"It must have been fearsome," Mossa agreed. "It makes me wonder, even, if the motivation—"

"Wait. Did that station have an andén for suspended railcars? Like this one?"

At that, she looked less smug. "I cannot be sure. I did not see one, or—" She closed her eyes, then resumed with more certainty. "Or anything that appeared to be the entrance to one. More convincingly, I would think the inhabitants, if they were aware of such a thing—and how could they not be, living on such a small space?—would have considered the possibility. But if it was long unused, they may have simply forgotten about it, and the entrance could have been from anywhere on the platform."

"Assuming there was one . . ."

"If there wasn't one, he would have indeed stepped off the edge of the platform."

To land on the roof of a swaying and ancient railcar. I shuddered.

"I wonder," Mossa said thoughtfully, "where the suspended railcar is now."

"Still traversing the unpopulated expanse of Giant, presumably."

Mossa, who had been examining the underside of the rail as if it might show tracks, turned her concentrated glare on me. "It is possible, of course, that Bolien has not yet arrived here. But if we are presuming anything, it should be that the railcar arrived and departed, and that someone is still on this platform. Perhaps it is unlikely—indeed, why would anyone stay, given the means to leave? But I'd rather be surprised by their absence than their presence." I nodded, chastened, and she swung towards the ramp. "Let's go ascertain one or the other."

Chapter 17

Early in the exile a number of people, arriving from energy-depleted Earth, went a bit wild at the idea of an enormous sphere composed largely of gas. They thought that they'd be returning to Earth soon enough, once science had solved everything or nature had healed itself, and some of them set about figuring ways to transport some of this bounty of energy back with them. I don't know if they were really still, at that point in human history, thinking about making themselves rich, or if it was in the interests of *everyone*'s unhealthy lifestyles that they were going to extract as much energy as they could manage to from *yet another* planet. Sometimes I agreed with Rechaure: *We deserve this lifeless planet.*

As time went on the possibility of returning to Earth, which at first seemed imminent to the congenitally rich and optimistic, receded, and most gas compression factories had been repurposed for something useful, like processing of foodstuffs. It was a little odd to see one abandoned instead, but it was remote and the square-meterage of the platform was not very large; most of the mechanical capacity was below our feet, extending down into the thicker gasses below us.

Even so, it gave me a womb-deep thrill of distaste to wander through this monument of wasted resources. "Why do people do such things?"

"You know why." Mossa's voice seemed to blend with the shadowy recesses of the factory.

"I know," I responded, "but I don't understand."

She didn't answer, and after a moment I looked over at her. The platform was very dim, lit only by the faint sunlight filtering through the fog, the atmoshield, and the long windows in the ceiling of the factory. Although the building was not large, the high ceiling and inexplicable bulks of machinery darkened its corners and long strips of its interior.

Nonetheless, I had felt confident that it was empty. The silence underlying the normal groans of wind and platform creaks was complete; I saw no movement, nothing flickering in even the deepest of shadows. We had an hour and twenty-seven minutes on this chilly platform while the railcar we had arrived on reached the westernmost station on this ring and returned on its journey east; if we missed that, it would be five hours before the next westbound railcar arrived. I was trying not to imagine that even Mossa could take longer than an hour and a half to search for clues in a moderately sized, empty building, however convoluted its furnishing. But now that I looked over at her, I could see she was intent on the wall to our left, in particular a patch of shadow near the middle, between two geometries of gasket, pipe, boxiness, and tube.

I opened my mouth to say her name, or perhaps ask what she was looking at, but fortunately my brain caught up with my action before I could speak, and I snapped it closed again. Mossa did not look at me, and yet I could feel her awareness as she edged silently towards the darker area. I moved sideways; if anyone was in there, they had probably seen us both already, but at least we could come at them from different angles.

The wind soughed its eerie unfurling howl outside the factory. The wind on Giant sounded very different from the wind on Earth: longer, steadier, intense. Early settlers apparently found it quite unnerving. To me, as it covered the light tap of our feet against the metal of the platform, it was almost comforting.

Mossa reached the crevice between the machines first. She paused for a slow breath and then whipped inside its shelter.

I followed quickly, but not quickly enough: as I rounded the angle to peer into the darkness I heard a shriek, and hurtled forward in time to see her feet disappear over the unexpectedly unwalled edge of the platform.

I was caught in shock for a moment, resisting the looming pressure of enormous grief, and then shook myself out of it and rushed towards the edge, with only enough caution to keep myself from plummeting over the side myself. Mossa would already have fallen past visibility, quickly claimed by the freezing fog and disappearing from sight long before she was crushed in on herself—but no! As I leaned over the edge, I could make out a darker shape in the dimness, and as my eyes adjusted there she was, suspended by the friction of her fingertips along the steep curving slope of a chute.

I exhaled: of course, with most of the factory's machinery below the platform, the atmoshield would extend below as well.

"Pleiti," Mossa gasped, breathless from the impact or the cold or the effort, "don't—"

Before she could finish telling me not to follow her, I dived in.

Whether by intention or because her frictive coefficient was giving out, Mossa disappeared downward before I reached her. The chute looped downward, long and bumpy enough that I had time to wonder whether I would be decanted into a furnace, compressor, or (unlikely in this type of facility, but such is imagination) table saw, but when I tumbled out of the slide it was to hit an unforgivingly hard surface, and in the time it took me to regain my breath I was neither roasted, nor crushed, nor sliced.

Despite the reassuring steadiness of the floor, a clanging and the sound of panting alerted me that the situation wasn't entirely peaceful. I wrenched myself up, pushing awkwardly to my feet, and in the almost impenetrable gloom saw Mossa rolling and kicking, and another figure above her, holding something which collected what little light there was into a gleam.

With a hoarse yell that I'm embarrassed to remember, I threw myself at them.

I was able to knock the knife-wielding person off their feet. They felt small but strong, with uncompromising arms that instead of fighting me away pulled me close. Wary of the sharp point somewhere on their person, I managed to work the sole of my foot between us and kick, but I couldn't get it high enough to get as much leverage as I needed to fully push them away. I was rewarded by a grunt, but almost immediately felt a thud and a burn along my arm. Then Mossa was slamming something into the stranger's head, knocking them away. I rolled onto my hands and knees, trying to breathe. One good breath, then I would get up and help Mossa. She would want to contain the person, not kill them, so that she could find out . . .

- - - - - - -

Chapter 18

I woke up in bed.

It was not my bed.

The clinic. I was aching and pained, but I did not feel anxious. I had been cared for, and my body knew it before I thought to ask the question.

No, I observed some time later, it was not the clinic. The furnishings, though plain, were too personal. The room was small, but when I moved my eyes from the ceiling I could see several shelves of books, their tabs sticking out somewhat haphazardly. The blanket tucked around me was warm and comfortingly soft. I was still drowsy. Then my eyes wandered down to the engraving on the wall by the slightly open door. It was an engraving of Io, based on an astronomical photograph taken by an uncrewed spacecraft during the Classical Era, and I knew every curve of it, for I had seen it often when—when Mossa and I shared rooms at university!

I was in Mossa's home.

I must have made some sound, as in my sudden energy I turned on the bed to look around, for a moment later the door swung quietly open and Mossa's peaked face leaned in. "Pleiti." She said it very quietly. "You're awake. I'm so glad." She stepped in, closed the door, and sat on the chair beside the bed—placed there and angled towards my pillow, I noticed, as if she had expected to sit there, or as if she already had.

"Have I been unconscious long?" I croaked, uncertain. I remembered the compression factory, the attack.

"Nearly a full day," she said. "But that is not from your injury, or not from your injury alone; I gave you stasis pills at the factory. I was afraid," she paused very slightly, her face seemed to waver in my vision, "I was afraid I would not be able to stop the bleeding in time, and we were far from any assistance."

"You carry *stasis pills*?"

"I am an Investigator," Moss reminded me austerely. "It is not such an uncommon need for me."

I let that disturbing acknowledgment pass. "Where are we?"

"In my rooms." She looked around, as though they were new to her too, although I was confident she could have told me the title of every book on that shelf, in whatever order I wished. "On Sembla."

I hadn't known where she lived. "We're not so far from Valdegeld," I said, attempting to sit up. "You could have . . ." Nausea accosted me and I hesitated, fighting the urge to vomit. Mossa offered a small basin, but I held up a hand—I could not afford to shake my head—and breathed as I had learned in my adaptation class, and it passed. "Could you—" I started, but she had already caught the meaning of my gesture and was arranging the pillows so that I could sit up more comfortably.

"I did not think Valdegeld would be wise," Mossa said, when I had settled. "We know of at least one conspirator there. Here we can recoup our energies and consider our next move."

"Mm," I said, because I had not meant to suggest that she could have brought me back to my own rooms; rather, I had been wondering why she hadn't visited me before. I swallowed the inadvisable question and covered by adjusting myself against the pillows. Terrible things, pillows: so soft and accommodating that they won't stay the way you want them for more than a few minutes. "What happened at the factory, after I—" I stopped, not sure how to convey *proved to be a weakness*.

"After you saved my life?" Mossa asked, and continued over my objection. "The attacker turned on you, but I was able to use that focus to take control of the situation. Once I had ascertained that you were not going to bleed to death immediately, I restrained our assailant."

I had expected something so different, it took me a moment to understand what she was saying. "You captured the person?"

"I did." Her tone was calm, but there might have been the faint suggestion of a crease at the corner of her mouth.

"Well?" I struggled to rise again, and the nausea was less this time. "What news?"

"I have not yet interrogated him. I was seeing to you first, and to my own needs, and in any case I thought the wait might be useful."

"Wait—he's *here*?"

"In the other room." Mossa blinked at me. "What did you expect?"

"Oh, I don't know, that you might hand the dangerous criminal over to the Investigators?"

"I am an Investigator."

"Well, yes, but . . ." I gestured helplessly. "I was under the impression that you—that Investigators, at least—sometimes worked with each other." That there were official places for interrogations to take place and prisoners to be held; that one might want some semblance of distinction between such work and one's privacy. Mossa, evidently, did not cherish her rooms as I did mine.

Although of course I worked in my rooms all the time.

Mossa raised a shoulder. She had changed her clothes—the ones she had been wearing at the factory must have been bloodstained, after she had dragged me all this way, including at least one railcar change. *And* with a prisoner. Had she given him a stasis pill too? "I will deposit him with my bureau once we know what we need to know. It seemed counterproductive to do so beforehand."

I decided not to question her office politics, which sounded like they must rival those of the university. "Well then," I said, with an effort towards robustness. "Shall we get started?"

That time I was sure I saw a smile. "You need some food first. I'll bring soup."

I wondered if she was enjoying the opportunity to offer me the same comfort I had given her. I rather thought so, and submitted with contentment to the careful palm on my forehead, the solicitous serving of the thick warming broth.

Chapter 19

I was much restored by the soup, and when Mossa offered me some clothes—my own, from her satchel—and stepped outside the room (on her own account; I wouldn't have asked it), I moved to dress myself without hesitation. I did have a moment of unease when I stood, but the stasis pill had done its work, along with the broth (I wondered then if perhaps she had dosed that with something as well). My arm was sore, and showed a long red streak from the knife, and it would probably take some time for the muscle to fully knit, but my head was clear and the rest of my body felt almost normally strong.

Mossa had packed me a selection of possible clothes. I decided that for interrogating a dangerous criminal the dressing gown was lacking in protection, and donned an ensemble I could have worn to my office.

Mossa was waiting for me in the hall. "Ready?"

I squirmed a little. "I'm not sure. Mossa, are we really about to . . . take this into our own hands, so to speak?"

She looked at me, face impassive, probably trying to understand what I was objecting to. "Whose hands would be better?"

I could only shrug at that, and after waiting for any other objection she led me into the next room.

As we walked in I was well into a meditation on the permissive uses of violence or restraint, and how the Classical World had differed on these points from our lives here on Giant; whether the professional fetters on the ankles of the man lying tied on the undyed rug were better or worse than something appropriated from another use. These philosophical thoughts were largely, though not completely, dispersed by the identity of the prisoner. I crouched by his head. "Bolien Trewl."

He raised his head to look at me and almost spat. "You! I should have known you were involved."

That seemed nonsensical, since I had been drawn in largely by the happenstance of knowing Mossa. "Involved?"

But he was still talking. "Wait, was that you in the factory? I should have hit you *harder.*" Then he really did spit. "Conservative that you are! You're too late, anyway."

I couldn't help flinching a little at the slur; it was not something I had ever been called or accused of being before. "You think I'm afraid of change because I want to keep the Preservation Institute open? You've done enough research there, Trewl, how could you sell them out?"

He just laughed at me, mouth twisted in scorn and hate. Mossa's hand came down on my shoulder, reminding me not to let him distract me from our purpose. "Who are you working with?" I asked.

His eyes flashed at me. "Working with?" It was an expression of disdain more than a question.

"Working with," I repeated. "Who met you at the factory? Where are the biological samples you stole?" Though I knew the samples were inert, I could not help hoping he had not simply tipped them off a platform somewhere.

He started to splutter again. Mossa leaned in over my shoulder. "Your confederate killed Rechaure."

Bolien started at that. "Re—Someone killed Rechaure?" He had started to say something else first, I was certain of it, but had caught it so quickly that I couldn't have sworn to whether it had been the beginning of an oath or the initial sound in a name. "Why would anyone do that? Old fellow wasn't a threat to anyone."

"You should think very carefully about whom you've chosen to work with." Mossa's voice was heavy with the prediction of betrayal and disaster, but Bolien didn't seem to notice.

"Nothing to do with me, and I'm sorry for it, but it's nothing to do with me and you can't possibly connect it. Rechaure was alive and ranting on his corner last time I left Valdegeld, and I've been pretty far away ever since." He smirked.

"And what exactly were you doing on the other side of the globe?"

He didn't seem surprised that we knew about his long journey, shrugging his shoulders against the rug. "Seeing the planet. Haven't you ever wanted to go around Giant?"

"It must have been a very shaky trip in a suspended rail-car," I commented.

"What good is an adventure if it's not a little uncomfortable?"

I was getting very tired of his smirk. I started naming the people I had found who seemed likely to undermine the

Preservation Institute, but he only laughed harder at each name, until he was coughing and choking on his spite. At last Mossa drew me gently out of the way. She tipped Bolien up into a sitting position until he had stopped choking, then kicked him down to the rug again and led me from the room with a nod.

"We'll give him some time," she said, in the hall. "A promenade, perhaps, Pleiti?"

She took her bag from a hook on the wall and, seeing my satchel beside it, I slung it on as well. I did not expect we'd be going far, but with Mossa I had learned to distrust my expectations.

Chapter 20

From the door of Mossa's rooms we proceeded down two stories of long ramp, and onto the street. "Radiation," I swore, as we stepped away from the building. "I'm terrible at interrogation."

"You're not expected to be good at it," Mossa replied, "with no training and no practice. But that's not the problem. I believe we're missing something from our theoretical narrative." It occurred to me, belatedly, that her fierce glower was a sign of intense concentration rather than a reflection of ire at my ineptitude. "Even accounting for bravado and an unusual level of arrogance and self-involvement, his lack of reaction at our questioning suggests that we are not threatening the core of whatever secret he is protecting." She was silent for a few moments, doubtless in an attempt to perceive the shape of this absent understanding, then, apparently recalling my existence, added, "I find that a stroll can be helpful—" She stopped suddenly, peered at me anxiously, "If you're not too tired? Or hurting? How is your arm?"

"I don't mind a walk," I said, and I didn't. I was looking around with interest. I had not spent much time in Sembla, for one thing, though I always enjoyed the newer city as a contrast to Valdegeld; and then again, I was interested to see the neighborhood where Mossa had decided to live.

Unlike Valdegeld, with its precipitous walls and tight streets, the remnants of a time when platforms—when any surface area at all—were desperately scarce, Sembla offered low buildings, accessible and spaced out. This platform was known for its gardens, little squares interspersed with the buildings, bedded with fine volcanic soil laboriously shuttled in from Io, and so every few minutes unexpected trees peeked at us through the early morning mist with flashes of beleaguered green.

"I suppose, if he tipped the cells into the planet, it's not like he has much to lose," I said at last. "And not much we can do about it in any case."

"I don't believe he did," Mossa said. "It is a lot of trouble to go for something so indirect as ruining the Preservation Institute. Surely there would be other ways? And even if there were not, if he *was* paid to do that, a man like that would not throw away anything potentially valuable. He would try to sell it, even with the risk. Or, I don't know, use them for his research."

"Perhaps you're right."

"More than that, though," Mossa went on, slipping her arm through mine to guide me into the next garden, "consider the suspended railcar."

I could consider nothing at that moment but the delicate

pressure of the crook of her elbow against mine. "The suspended railcar?"

Mossa had always hated senseless repetition of phrases, but she answered without irritation. "The one Bolien traveled around Giant on. It wasn't waiting in the station below."

"It took someone else off, then! Of course, you had suggested something of the sort when we saw the empty andén." I turned to her, then regretted it when she removed her arm. "But how was he going to leave?"

"I imagine on the railcar we came in on. I must have frightened him off when I disembarked so quickly. Why else would he have been hiding in that factory?"

"Of course," I said, chagrined not to have seen it myself.

Mossa smiled at me. "I did have a head start in considering these questions while you were unconscious."

The park we were in was walled, to better protect the foliage from storms, and though it was probably little larger than my set of rooms at Valdegeld, the dense shrubbery and twisting paths made it seem obscure and mysterious, as though we could lose ourselves, and between the thorny tangles it was almost warm.

"It's lovely here," I said, inconsequentially but honestly.

Mossa made a little huffing sound. "It's not Valdegeld."

Again, I turned to look at her; she was scowling. "It's far more pleasant than Valdegeld in many ways."

"Yes, it's convenient here, and there are—" She indicated the foliage with a sharp wave of the hand. "But it doesn't have, oh, the craggy plenitude of history in its glorious variegation of architectural styles or the august air of academia pervading its atmoshield—"

"I don't know which guidebooks you're quoting," I

sputtered, laughing, "but they're terrible! And yes, I'm very fond of Valdegeld, but—" I intended to say something like *Sembla is also wonderful* or *it's pleasant to have a change now and again*. But I looked at her face, eager and frowning, and instead I said, "But I'm also very fond of you."

Mossa's expression was like the one she had worn in theoretical forestry class when the professor had offered successively more difficult elimination problems until Mossa, alone, had comprehended the final paradigm: as though I were as fascinating and satisfying to grasp as her most difficult questions. But then she shook her head.

"Pleiti," she said. "I haven't changed."

"Haven't changed? What do you mean you haven't changed?" She hadn't changed her mind about me? About Valdegeld and my work and . . .

"Since university."

I laughed. I think at the same time I took her hand, or perhaps I already had. "Mossa. You have certainly changed since university."

"When we . . . when you . . . said you didn't want a romantic relationship with me any more. In university." As though I could have forgotten when we were together. "You said that I was oblivious, and hard-hearted, and put too much value on personal attachment to work and not enough on the greater good, and—"

"I—" I couldn't think how to answer that.

"And it's true, that's still all true! And you're a scholar at *Valdegeld* just like you always dreamed of being and you are doing important work about getting us back to Earth—" Something pinged in the back of my mind at that, but I had no time for the back of my mind in that moment.

"Mossa. Mossa. *You* are doing important work. And—

and—I don't know anything about Investigator culture, but I could tell your colleagues respect you, admire you even. And you have your own home in this beautiful city. You *have* changed since university, even if not exactly in the way I—And mostly—mostly I don't care."

"You don't?"

I should have, I knew that, but I couldn't. "I don't."

"Does that mean—do you mean—Pleiti, might I kiss you?"

"Yes," I said in a rush, and threw my arms around her.

Chapter 21

We had arrived, somehow, in a small sward (as such places used to be called) in the interior of the garden, where the vegetation was not encouraged to grow above knee level and a small bench, to one side, suggested quiet contemplation of the remnants of another planet's nature.

I contemplated Mossa (who was also, after all, a remnant of another planet's nature). This gambit was, I knew, foolish. As she said, she had not changed, not in the ways that had made our relationship impossible so many years ago. She was unromantic, focused on her own unusual intellect, distant, and uninterested in the issues I was passionate about. And I was a scholar at Valdegeld, a situation both privileged and precarious, with the hope of contributing, in some marginal, probably not even footnoted way, to the grand project that was the resettlement of Earth . . .

Mossa's lips found a sensitive spot on the side of my neck, and with a shiver of delight I folded away those uncomfortable vectors of thought for the moment.

In the next pause, however, they returned. I had little idea of the work schedule of an Investigator, although these past few days she had certainly seemed mistress of her own time. Was it possible she might—I cut off the thought, and returned my attention to her delectable ear, the softness of her hair . . .

Then again, the way she had captured—captured!— Bolien, a colleague of mine no less, even if one that I thoroughly disliked, it was disturbing, such actions and such license . . . My thoughts were confused, and I rested my eyes on our surroundings. A cricket chirped from somewhere in the briars. Mossa laid her head on my shoulder with a soft sigh. A small goshawk hit the ground a scant meter away, scrabbled in the dirt, cast a lightning glare at us, and lofted again, disappearing quickly into the murk. I followed its leap, fascinated; on Valdegeld we did not have goshawks, only pigeons.

On platforms where goshawks had been brought, pigeons never lasted, torn to bits before they could propagate. On one place, I heard, they reanimated a hundred pigeons at once—I don't know why anyone would be so set on having pigeons, of all things, some romantic Earth notion—but the goshawks were too well established already (goshawks having been another romantic Earth notion, one particularly widespread at the time when animals were being introduced on Giant), and wrecked the pigeons in no time.

It was a common problem; it had happened on Earth multiple times, with invasive species unbalancing ecosystems; it had happened during humanity's brief sojourn on Mars, and had contributed to making that planet, already ravaged by mining and extraction, as uninhabitable as

Earth. It was, in fact, the reason for my work, the reason
we were so careful . . .

"Mossa!" I was gasping already, my body hollowed by
the certainty, the inevitability of it, an insight as sudden
as the goshawk's stoop. She looked up, startled. "Mossa,"
I couldn't seem to get any other words out. "The list!" Not
enough, not even for her. "The list of stolen cells. From the
Preservation Institute! Do you have it?"

She rummaged in her bag. She had her bag; I had my
satchel, with the timetable: we could leave at once. I started
walking almost before she handed me the list and she followed. "What is it?"

I scanned it, then handed it back to her. "I'll explain on
the railcar. We have to go now. The nearest station?"

"Do we need to bring Bolien?"

"No. He wasn't going to tell us anything anyway; I can't
imagine he'll be helpful now." In truth, I couldn't bear to
spend a long ride with him tied up and smirking at us, or
worse still, in stasis. "Um . . . is there any way you can . . ."
Dislike him I might, but I couldn't countenance leaving
him alone and constrained on Mossa's floor.

"I'll send a telegram from the station," Mossa said with
a nod, and then took the lead, walking even faster than I
had, because she trusted me before I explained.

When we reached the station I studied the departure
board and the timetable while she ran to the telegraph office. By the time she returned I had selected an andén and
was tapping foot and fingertips with impatience. Mossa
glanced up at the list of stations on the route but said nothing, bless her. "All sorted?" I asked.

"Yes. I sent to the station, asked a colleague who has

my key to collect him." I had nothing to say to that, which somehow caused her to keep talking. "She—we—were in a relationship. Before. That's why she has my key. Not any more."

I smiled involuntarily: Mossa, nervous. About—could it be? Yes, it seemed the only interpretation—*me*.

"That seems reasonable," I said. "I take it it didn't cause problems for your working relationship?"

"No." Mossa sounded relieved. "Not at all. It was a very . . ." The pause stretched an improbably long time. "That is, rather . . ." She trailed off a second time, with even more relief, as the railcar appeared along the distant reach of ring.

Chapter 22

It was, unfortunately, about an hour after dawn, and a number of people who commuted across the Sembla-Arkenist-Pyl corridor were traveling as their days began, so our compartment was crowded. At Arkenist Mossa, with admirable foresight or perhaps uncontrollable hunger, sprang out to buy a pair of food packets from a station vendor. When she handed me the odorous packet I discovered that I, too, needed to eat, and consumed it, shoulders hunched beside the other passengers. It was not until we had left the bustling station of Pyl that we were finally alone in our compartment.

Mossa waited until we had been out of the station long enough to be fairly certain no latecomers would stumble into our isolation. "Do we have some time?"

"Some hours yet," I said, suddenly wearied by the massive secret I was carrying. It wasn't that I didn't want to tell Mossa: indeed, passing it into her competent hands might be the only thing that would offer some relief. And yet, the idea of saying it out loud conjured a deep reluctance.

Her eyes went distant, and I knew she was reviewing the list of stations on this line, then connections, trying to understand where we were going. But there was no flicker of insight, and I roused myself. "It's—" Still difficult to say. I pulled out the list she had given me in the garden. "Look. The biomaterials are in no kind of order here—or perhaps it's an order that makes sense to the mauzooleum workers, based on where the habitats are located or something of the sort. But if we think instead of the relationships between the animal and plant *species . . .*" I waited, hoping she would see it. It was a long list, though, and her eyes darted up and down it for some moments before I saw them widen.

"You think—this could be an ecosystem?"

"An attempt at one, in any case." I swallowed against the dryness of my throat. "Bolien—you were right about him, this was more than just attacking the Preservation Institute. That's why he laughed so hard, he realized we didn't know. His theories, about altitude—he would be able to put a list together, for a specific location on Earth."

This time, her whole expression changed with the shock of it. "You think they're going to send these to *Earth*?"

I nodded, my arms curled around my stomach. "They'll send them, and—and, if they're a little bit lucky, and hit the right place and have planned the rocket kit correctly, it could happen. They'll restart life on Earth with this set of animals and—and all our work—every scholar, every hour of study, all the planning, all our *care*—" I doubled over in the seat, and a hesitant few seconds later Mossa's hand was rubbing my shoulders.

"Surely," she started, and then thought better of it. "Even if they start this in one area, that can't obviate the plans for the whole planet?"

"It could. It—there are so many factors, Mossa. That's why we're being so careful, studying the exact proportions that *worked,* back before we managed to fuck it up. Starting from zero like that is one thing. But trying to integrate with an existing ecosystem, even one that's limited to one area . . . I don't know." Telling her *had* helped: I was already starting to feel a whisper of hope. "Maybe. I'll talk to the rest of the scholars, the research directors, the dean of the Classics faculty . . ."

"That's *if* we don't stop them," Mossa said. "I take it we're going to Uliram?" It was the only spaceport with facilities, rarely enough used for anything but probes, for extra-orbital travel.

"They've probably left already," I said glumly.

"Perhaps not," Mossa replied. She tugged gently at my head and I rested it on her shoulder. "There. The suspended railcars are somewhat slower, and perhaps they had some other preparations to make. We shall see what we find. And if they have, we will face that too." She continued rubbing my shoulder for a long time, until well after my tears had stopped, and even then she simply adjusted my position to her chest so she could lean back more comfortably, and we stayed that way, her arm around me. The comfort of it was sweeter than her kisses had been, and that was very sweet indeed.

Chapter 23

As we approached Uliram, my mood became more optimistic. "Surely the officials at the spaceport will have stopped them from departing? It's not so easy to just walk in and commandeer a rocket."

"Hmm." Mossa's countenance was not sanguine, and at the next stop her skepticism was, if not borne out, given support. While we paused at the station—it was Jarbin, a large enough platform for the railcar to pause several minutes before departing—an attendant dashed on board, glancing from compartment to compartment until he could thrust the telegram flimsy into Mossa's waiting hands and then dive back onto the andén even as the railcar gave its premonitory shudder.

Mossa looked the message over and then handed it to me. "My colleague," she said, with only a slight hesitation. Her impervious carapace was closing over her again. "When I sent the telegram from Sembla station I asked her to follow up on certain things and send anything relevant to me along this ring."

The message read:

Notable absence from Valdegeld on dates specified only Rector Spandal

"Someone of that stature," Mossa remarked as I stared at it, "would stand a good chance of suborning or simply blustering over any opposition."

I looked up, appalled. "Surely not!"

"Is the rector a strong supporter of the Classics faculty?"

I started to answer, and had to stop. I was, in truth, too many rungs below the rector to have direct interaction with him in the subtle spheres of university politics. But Mossa's question brought to mind a multitude of offhand comments, a subtle antagonism, a number of suggestions, carefully couched in the academic discourse, that the grand project of the Classical department might be *taking too long*.

"But even so . . . this . . . unethical . . . utterly . . . beyond . . ." I realized I was spluttering, and took a breath. When I had sorted my outrage, what came out of my mouth was: "This is a man with so much power in the academic world. Why would he need to do something so appallingly underhanded?"

Mossa responded simply with a Classical quotation: "'Why are men?'"

"Granted, but even so. This man could have hindered or hurried our work in any number of ways . . ." I stopped again, this time to consider whether he *had*, subtly enough that we hadn't even noticed, and then leaving that aside went on. "How could he excuse stealing biological samples, undermining the collective decision process of all of Giant, not to mention murdering poor Rechaure?"

"With any luck, you'll have the chance to ask him." Mossa pointed out the window and there, looming out of the fog ahead of us, I saw the massive spire of a rocket signaling our approach to the spaceport.

- - - - - - - -

Chapter 24

Uliram platform was exclusively dedicated to the spaceport: there were no living quarters and only the most minimal of administration, both of those being consigned to other platforms nearby (but not too nearby) so as to reduce any casualties from accidental explosions, or even from the entirely intentional consequences of a rocket launch powered by a focused explosion that channeled fuel from the planet into combustion within the platform, rather than in the rocket itself as in spaceflight from Earth.

But while it wasn't entirely unusual that there was no one on the station's solitary andén, no one at all, it was still unsettling. And when the gate into the spaceport was also unguarded, I began to worry that Mossa had been correct. "Mossa . . ."

"Hurry," she urged me over her shoulder.

"But Mossa," I said, panting slightly as we charged along the narrow labyrinth of blast walls that would eventually lead us to the launching pad, "if we arrive at the moment of launch . . ."

"We will hear—and probably feel—the machinery for the focusing and calibration of the explosion long before ignition," Mossa assured me, still half-running several paces ahead; apparently rocket science was yet another area in which she had acquired some expertise. "Ah! You feel that vibration?"

In all honesty, I did not, but as that was probably due to my pounding heartbeat and both our footsteps echoing in the narrow corridors I took her word for it. "How . . . long . . . does that . . . leave us?"

"At least twenty minutes. There's a wide range of force and directionality that need to be precisely—ah!"

We had emerged into the first of the broad open launch pads. This one, however, was empty. "Could he have launched it already?"

Mossa did not bother to answer, sprinting instead towards the far wall.

I trailed her across three unoccupied launch areas, each roofless but for the atmoshield and open onto the wheeling moons, I followed her through the doubling, layered corridors between them, as the vibration of the launch mechanism augmented around us until even I could hear the reverberations rumbling the walls and floor.

On the fourth launch pad we found a rocket.

It was smaller than I had expected, but menacingly armored all the same. From the many theoretical diagrams I had seen, I recognized the nose cone specially designed to disintegrate and distribute frozen cells in reanimation packets. "He's really doing it," I panted.

Mossa, who had finally stopped running (and, to my

gratification, was at least breathing heavily) nudged my arm and jerked her chin towards the console near the base of the spaceship and the figure poring over it.

I forgot my exhaustion and for once outpaced Mossa in my fury. Fortunately the roar of the launch mechanism had grown distractingly loud, and Rector Spandal—for indeed it was he—was not aware of me until I grabbed his stooped and august shoulder and yanked him away from the panel.

His brows cranked together in fury, but otherwise his face was blank: he didn't recognize me. And why should he? I was only an unimportant myrmidon among thousands, pouring my time and effort and imagination into a project that he had decided he disagreed with, or couldn't wait for. I was so choked by this, and he so surprised by my gall in appearing much less accosting him, that neither of us had managed to say anything before Mossa's cry rang out: "Sembla Investigators Bureau, holding you to account for the murder of the person known as Rechaure—"

"What!" the rector bellowed: not even a question, just outrage.

"And conspiracy in the theft of biological materials from the—"

"Theft? I'll have you know—"

"—misuse in unsanctioned rocket launch—"

"I have perfect authority—"

"How dare you?" I screamed across them both. I was jabbing my finger at the rocket. "You are going to overturn years, *decades* of planning for Earth reanimation, delay the time when we can *finally* go back—"

"Delay?" Rector Spandal turned fully to me, swaying with the force of his anger or self-justification. "*Delay?* You

Classics fools would *never* have decided! You would *never* be ready to start! Believe me, I have been waiting, expecting that resettlement might happen in my lifetime or in my son's lifetime, but you—"

"And you will push it off for decades if not centuries more!" I yelled at him. "With this precipitate, irresponsible, *selfish* action, you will distort the evolution of—"

"It's never going to be Earth!" It was almost a screech. "Not the Earth that you *Classicists* deify! It's never going to be exactly like it was before, and that means you're never going to be willing to let us get back there." He leaned forward, grabbing my shirt and pulling. "So happy here, studying your ancient texts and cozy in those ridiculous quarters *we* give you, no wonder you don't feel any urgency! Well, young lady, I don't care what you think should happen. *I* am going to the planet I am *supposed* to be living on!"

"You're *going*?" The absolute lack of hinges in his plan blotted over all his insults: I simply couldn't believe it. "You're physically going to . . ."

"Earth." The rector straightened his back, then his clothing. "You're welcome to keep dreaming about a meta-ecosystem that is gone forever while I breathe air and swim in water and—"

"It's not ready," I said, suddenly desperate to save this stupid, overbearing man's life. "You're going to be breathing poison, swimming in poison—"

"So they tell us," he said. "I'm going to find out."

"You're not going anywhere." Mossa had a whip-lasso out, the Investigator's non-lethal tool. "I'm going to ask you once to stop that rocket of your own—"

"Mossa!" I screamed, as Professor Porbal charged out of the dimness behind her, his arms pulled back in the wind-up for a swing with what I saw, as it came around, was a metal object. A pipe, maybe, or a wrench. I should have yelled *duck*. For months after I would wake up sweating and wishing I had, but perhaps I wasn't sure enough of his angle of attack in time and perhaps it wouldn't have mattered.

Mossa was at least fast enough in turning towards him that the club caught her across the face instead of on the back of her skull. Blood sprayed horribly and I dove for Porbal—that, too, how had it not occurred to me that this person we *knew* to be part of the conspiracy might be there, that the mad rector was not entirely alone?—and drove him to the ground. I looked up in time to see Rector Spandal shove a key into the control panel, turn it, and then pull it out. He glanced in our direction once, his face garish in the glow of the indicators, twisted with scornful laughter, the hand with the key clasped in a hard fist. Then he took off running towards the rocket ship.

I was still struggling with Porbal. He had landed under me, but he was gripping the pipe, and he nearly got a bash in with it before I caught his wrist with both my hands. I worked my knee in under his ribs while we struggled, he pushed at me with his free hand and tried to get it at my face, but despite my inability to keep up with Mossa during our sprint earlier, I do bolster my academic lifestyle with *some* exercise; if nothing else, the stairs to my room had tempered my quads. I was able to push his weapon hand to the platform and bring my foot up to step on it until he let go; I got in a few additional kicks as I stood, and left him stunned enough that I had time to grab for Mossa's whip-lasso and lash it around him. (I had never before realized how pleasurable those weapons are to handle: the flick of the wrist, the satisfying contraction of the cords around the target. I had to admire Mossa's restraint in not using it more.)

Mossa was lying on the ground, her split cheek open to the sky, her eyes blinking but unfocused. "Mossa," I whispered, that quiet echo already awash with the guilt of my misused last cry to her. "Are you well? Can you move?"

She blinked again and murmured something, but it was no clearer than the syllables of a sleeping lover, sounds that seem to be coherent words but are impossible to decipher. Mossa used to speak so in her dreams, in university when we shared a bed.

I rubbed away my tears. Porbal was lying, cursing, a few feet away from us; the platform was vibrating thunderously; and as I slipped my hands under Mossa's head, thinking to cradle it gently on my lap, a pre-recorded voice further shook the hangar: "Launch," it proclaimed, in the timpani accents that signaled *educated* when this spaceport was built and now sounded archaic, "in ten minutes."

Chapter 25

I somehow shuffled Mossa to her feet, but she leaned so heavily it was more like carrying her, and I begrudged every jostle and bump that thumped her head against my shoulder. I had nothing left for Porbal but one hand, and I caught the user end of the whip-lasso and dragged him after us, my recently stabbed arm protesting each step, while he shrieked. It wasn't until we had nearly crossed the launch pad that I realized he was screaming not, as my guilt had assumed, because I was scraping him against the platform, but because I was taking him away from the rocket.

"Let me go~~~~~~~!" he wailed. "I was supposed to go~~~~! Please, please—" and then he devolved into a sobbing so pitiful that I might have questioned my decision if Rector Spandal had shown the least inclination to stop and pull him up on the rocket instead of incinerating him on the platform; if I hadn't been too desperate to escape to pause for even a moment; and, of course, if he hadn't tried to kill Mossa.

As it was, I got him through the entirety of the first blast wall—fortunately, there were quick exit paths designed for emergencies, I don't know if I could have lugged them both through the entrance maze—and deserted him on the next launch pad. The blast walls were there to protect contiguous launch areas, I assured myself: the spaceport could not have been designed to destroy itself with every launch (*although,* a counter-argument whispered, *most launches were simple shuttles into orbit; this interplanetary attempt might be more damaging?*). He had been screaming for me to let him go for the last forty seconds (precisely timed by the ten-second intervals of countdown warnings); in any case, I could not manage the two of them any longer. I loosed the whip-lasso, my cramped hand struggling to let go, and lifted Mossa with both arms, a weight but a dearer one, and my strength burgeoned anew. Porbal was by that time too exhausted to yell, but his sobbing followed us across that terrible space until the door of the next blast wall closed behind us.

If Mossa's weight in my arms had seemed negligible after the shuffle-drag of the first launch pad, by the time we were halfway through the last I could barely stagger under it. My atmoscarf had slipped down, and the harsh admixture of oxygen stung my heaving lungs. We had entered the final two minutes of countdown. I was almost certain we were safe from the explosion, but some atavistic part of me, doubtless genetically encoded during the violent ages of Earth, refused to believe it and insisted on reaching the station as soon as possible. The mirage of a railcar, doors open and ready to speed us along its ring, urged me onward, but when I finally reached the station, finding it empty and the next railcar not due for another nine minutes, it was almost a relief: there was no more I could do. I sank down to the floor of the station, slid Mossa somewhat more gently under a bench, and followed, arranging myself above her.

It is possible she said something coherent at that point, but I couldn't make it out above my panting. "It's going to be fine, everything's going to be fine," I said between gasps, or something of the sort. "Just a few more minutes. It's going to be—" I don't know how many times I repeated that before it was cut off by the explosion.

The platform shook hard enough to revive my childhood fear of the entire planet igniting, but when there was no corresponding rush of heat I foolishly twisted enough to lean my head out from under the bench, tilted towards the sky. The engineering parameters of the spaceport seemed to have been adequate: there was no fire, no falling debris, and as I looked up past the edge of the station roof, I saw the rocket crease the heavens on its way towards Earth.

Chapter 26

It was a wearisome few days of convincing aghast officials of increasing prominence what had been done and that, however difficult they found it to believe this fact, it had been Rector Spandal who had done it. I heard any number of improbable explanations for the rector's empirical absence and drank many liters of tea before acceptance, of the events if not of their implications, finally reached a critical mass. I thought at that time I could retire to my rooms for several hot baths and perhaps two days of sleep, but my mere presence at the unknotting of the plot, happenstance though it was, somehow meant that my opinion was crucial to all that followed; I was required in meeting after meeting, briefing after briefing, all the various attempts to explicate and extrapolate the consequences in front of various positions of leadership, all of it time that I couldn't spend at Mossa's side while she was treated for the concussion and the broken cheekbone. When they insisted that I participate in the search for a new rector, I realized that, through the strange alchemy of proximity to significance, my status at the university had irrevocably changed.

Porbal did survive, although his hearing was somewhat damaged; still, it was a deep relief to me when they told me he had been found alive. He and Bolien were played against each other in the typical fashion, and in the typical fashion of individuals who believe the world should bend itself to their convenience, they sold each other out neatly, although they did try to crush Rector Spandal with much of the blame. According to Porbal, it was the rector who had loosed the caracal on us in the mauzooleum; Porbal said Spandal had told him about it afterwards, laughing at it as a foolish scheme, but one that he couldn't quite resist attempting. All three men had been convinced they would be able to survive on Earth while an ecosystem grew up around them.

Valdegeld (represented in part by yours truly), the Investigators, and the Earth Resettlement Authority were able to get a probe launched in record time, two days after the rector departed. It will follow his rocket, if slightly more slowly, and go into orbit around the planet, hopefully sending back images to confirm the fate of the rector and, more importantly, that of the additional biological material he took with him.

During the discussions pertinent to this launch—which, record time or no, felt nearly interminable—I could not prevent my thoughts drifting. Yes, it was vital work, but it was also so obvious that I had little patience with the details. When I wasn't looping historical or speculative moments with Mossa, I found myself conjuring an alternate life on Earth. It was difficult: I would imagine leaving a house, seeing grass and soil, and then I would realize that I had imagined myself wearing an atmoscarf. *Breathe air, swim in water,* the Rector had said, and the words twined into my brain: would living on the planet we had evolved for relax muscles I didn't know I was tensing? Then again, we had, largely on purpose, wrenched Earth into a very different state than that we had evolved for; would it really be so welcoming? If returning meant making all the adjustments of exile again, was it so worth it?

Not the same Earth; he had said that too. I wanted to believe that I had known always that *of course* the reseeded Earth would not be . . . not *exactly* the same, anyway. It still hurt to hear it said, hurt with a terrible epigenetic ache for an ecosystem I had never known but wanted, always wanted.

It will, of course, be some months yet before either of the ships arrive at their destination. There was some talk of sending an additional crewed ship, with its own payload of carefully selected species, as a sort of counterweight to the rector's less comprehensive approach. The argument was that a few days, or weeks even, would not make much difference, and the serious Classics scholars could wrest some control back and make the experiment more viable and aligned with our principles. However, the scholars involved have not reached an accord on the precise selection of species to send, and the Speculative biologists collaborating on the problem agree the window is closing.

It was this last development that drove me, if not to despair, then at least out of the meeting, down to the station, and on to the railcar to Sembla. As with every time I boarded a railcar, I remembered that day at the spaceport: hauling Mossa back to her feet after the explosion and half-dragging her forward as I watched the timer with an irrational worry that the railcar wouldn't arrive; my relief when I saw it, approaching exactly as scheduled; the expressions on the faces of the other passengers when we struggled on to the carriage . . . I shook my head, dismissing the images. Surely these flashbacks would fade with time. To assist with that I had brought a book for the journey: nothing Classical, a Modern saga set here on Giant.

In Sembla I walked slowly to Mossa's place. She had told me to come at any time; she did go for walks occasionally (I imagined her in that garden, *our* garden, where we had kissed), but as with every time I visited I wondered if someone else might be there; that "colleague" with her key, perhaps . . .

But as every previous time I had visited, Mossa was alone. There was a book—a Classical novel—on the table and the remnants of a storyboard on the wall, but when I asked what she had been doing she grumbled about the amount of paperwork required to close up the case.

"It's not closed, though," I blurted out. "We don't know what will happen to Spandal, or what will happen to Earth . . ."

Unexpectedly, she reached out an arm, and I moved to sit next to her, against her. She had been doing such things more often, but it still surprised me, every time. I told her about the meeting, and the stalemate, and she listened, but seemed hesitant to speak.

"This is why he called me a—the c-word," I said at last, sniffling. I had started crying as I spoke, and hadn't completely stopped yet. "We want everything to be perfect, to be the way it was, and that's . . . we're never going to find it. And so we'll never do anything. We'll never decide. Maybe—" I couldn't bring myself to say aloud that Spandal might have been right.

Mossa started rubbing my back, her face thoughtful.

"The Classics faculty may be a little . . . hidebound," she said cautiously, "but Spandal was wrong too. Attempting to approximate an idealized past is most certainly both futile and foolish, but individually disrupting what absolutely must be a collective endeavor is no better, and selfish as well."

"But what then? Do we stay here forever?" As I spoke, I recalled the other thing Spandal had said: *So happy here, studying your ancient texts and cozy in those ridiculous quarters.* It had been an attack, I knew: it had shivered me with guilt in the moment and every time I remembered it. But was it really so terrible? Yes, I loved my cozy quarters and ancient texts. My breathing calmed just thinking of it, of the students, and the operetta I had tickets for in a few days, and the easy railcar ride here to see Mossa. Was that enough, if there was no grand project of return?

Mossa, meanwhile, was answering what should have been an impossible bit of rhetoric. "I am sure there are approaches that fall into neither of those traps." From someone else, I would have thought those empty comforting words, but I could see that Mossa's mind was already gnawing at what those approaches might be. "Perhaps there's a discipline, or trans-discipline, of flexibility and reactiveness, or a calculation of the principles involved in ecosystem survival rather than the literal mimicking of known successes."

I inhaled the deepest breath I had managed since the goshawk.

"And you should work on it," she concluded.

"*Me?*" I had been immensely relieved by the reanimation of my hopes, I was unprepared to be praised as well.

"Yes, you. You're very open to thinking in new ways."

I looked at Mossa skeptically.

She returned the glance severely. "You are certainly not co—" She stopped, as reluctant as I to use that vicious epithet Bolien had thrown at me.

"I'm not?"

"No. Look at how quickly you adapted to helping with my investigation," she pointed out.

"Oh," I said softly, and then went on, headlong, with an utter absence of lyricism or subtlety: "And you're the greatest Investigator."

"Really?" I expected laughter, given how clumsy a compliment it had been, but she said it wonderingly, as if she believed me or tried to.

Still, I thought I could do better. "Really." I sat up properly, wiping my eyes. "I think I could adapt to a few other things, too," I said.

"Oh?" She eyed me cautiously.

"Like visiting Sembla. It's not so far from Valdegeld."

"No," Mossa said, with a hesitant smile, "it's not. I might visit Valdegeld as well."

I let her hold me for a while, the smile blooming on my face even though she couldn't see it.

"Mossa? When you said before, that you hadn't changed? In the ways I wanted you to?"

"Yes?"

"You have changed, you know. But even if you haven't changed everything that I said, back when—well. You don't need to. It doesn't matter."

"It does, though, it mattered to you a lot then—"

"It doesn't. You don't need to change. Because I have."

Acknowledgments

This book was written at a time of isolation and intensity. I am so appreciative of all the online connections that nurtured me. Thank you to the groups on Slack and Discord that invited me in, offered care and conversation, and modeled thoughtful, committed, voluntary approaches to the difficult work of building and maintaining healthy communities. Thank you to the scholars who reached out to collaborate across continents, disciplines, and time zones; thank you to the bookstores and writers, universities and nonprofits, who organized online events. Thank you to the theaters that streamed recorded performances or developed hybrid models and interactive experiments; thank you to the conferences that put time and resources into making it possible to share ideas and experiences without sharing contamination vectors; thank you to the fic writers on AO3, thank you to the public libraries that set up systems for borrowing and returning books from great distances. Thank you to the Twitter mutuals who interacted with respect and restraint and shared their expertise and interests, thank you to friends and family and followers still on Facebook who checked in and shared joy and organized play readings and poetry workshops. Thank you to everyone who decided to schedule a Zoom or Skype just to chat (and respected those times when one or more of the participants were Zoomed out).

Let's not lose what we learned about connecting across distance.

Thank you to all the writers whose accumulated, stored efforts sustained me during this time and gave me hope, comfort, and beauty. I will inevitably forget some, but in the interests of offering recommendations to others as well as offering gratitude (and in no particular order), thank you to Martha Wells, KJ Charles, T. Kingfisher (and, for that matter, Ursula Vernon), Sherry Thomas, Annalee Newitz, Naomi Kritzer, Laurie R. King, Charlie Jane Anders, Sarah Rees Brennan, Talia Hibbert, Karen Lord, Hilary Mantel, Freya Marske, Arkady Martine, Judith Flanders, Alexis Hall, Courtney Milan, Kelly Robson, Megan Whalen Turner, Elin Gregory, Katherine Addison, Zen Cho, Rabih Alameddine, Sarah Pinsker, Theresa Rebeck, Anne Perry, Henry Lien, Hilary McKay, Roan Parrish, Louise Penny, Olivia Atwater, Ann Leckie, Nicola Griffith, Shannon Hale, William Gibson, Kerry Greenwood, Nancy Springer, Stephanie Burgis, C. M. Waggoner, Andrea Beaty, Naomi Novik, Lee Welch, Y. S. Lee, Ben Aaronovitch, Casey McQuiston, Rosalie Knecht, Keigo Higashino, and many, many more. (NB: Please note that while I found works by these authors comforting and engrossing, some of them write a range of genres/subjects including *much less comforting ones* and, of course, comfort is subjective.)

Many people helped to make this book better, most importantly Brent Lambert, who not only edited it but also understood it, cheered it on, and pushed it to improve.

Thank you also to Emily Goldman, who guided this book through the publishing process with care and attention; Amanda Hong for copy editing and Andrea Wilk for proofing; Christine Foltzer, who designed the incredible cover; Natassja Haught and Michael Dudding for marketing; Saraciea Fennell (The Bronx is Reading! Latinx in Publishing!) and Jocelyn Bright for publicity; Samantha Friedlander for social media support; Lauren Hougen, Greg Collins, and Jim Kapp; and Irene Gallo.

Particular thanks to my very early readers, Dora Vázquez Older, Carmen Crow Sheehan, and Annahita de la Mare, for all your support, encouragement, and useful comments. Also to my slightly later readers, Charlie Jane Anders, Fran Wilde, KJ Charles, and Freya Marske, for your thoughtful reviews and your support.

Big thanks to Lale Uribe, for offering in-person friendship and empathy when I really needed it; to Carmen Crow Sheehan for steadfast friendship and finding ways to make long-distance support tactile as well as virtual with mini-care packages even under very difficult circumstances; and to Dora Vázquez Older, Marc Older, and Daniel José Older for finding ways to stay close. Thank you to Calyx, Paz, and Azul for everything.